Cry Riot!

Spargo was a mining town… but there hadn't been any mining there for a while. The mines were in a dangerous condition, and their owner, Foley Kingston, refused to make improvements. So the miners – those who'd survived the numerous cave-ins and accidents – went on strike, and Kingston called on his old friend, Duke Benedict, to help him break it.

Benedict's partner, big Hank Brazos, immediately sided with the miners. And even though Benedict knew Kingston was at fault, he had to stand by him. Back in the War, Kingston had saved his life, so he owed the man.

But there were darker forces at work in Spargo – from Kingston's cheating wife Rhea to saloon owner Ace Beauford, who wanted to run the entire outfit all by himself. And then there was a man-mountain named Paddy Clancy, who figured to double-cross all of them!

Cry Riot!

E. Jefferson Clay

A Black Horse Western

ROBERT HALE

First published by Cleveland Publishing Co. Pty Ltd,
New South Wales, Australia
First published in 1967
© 2020 Mike Stotter and David Whitehead

This edition © The Crowood Press, 2020

ISBN 978-0-7198-3122-5

The Crowood Press
The Stable Block
Crowood Lane
Ramsbury
Marlborough
Wiltshire SN8 2HR

www.bhwesterns.com

Robert Hale is an imprint
of The Crowood Press

Typeset by
Simon and Sons ITES Services Pvt Ltd
Printed and bound in Great Britain by
4Bind Ltd, Stevenage, SG1 2XT

ONE

AMBUSH IN THE SUN

Murphy eased the Winchester forward as the three riders came into sight below. He grimaced as the sun caught fire along the barrel. Taking an experimental sighting, he framed the head of the middle horse in the cleft of the back sight and gently raised the front sight up into the notch. The blade danced as he looked over it at the rider's face. He saw a tall, dandyish looking hombre on a flashy black horse. Not him, he decided; he didn't look like a big-time man-killer.

The gunsights swung to the rider on the right—a giant on an appaloosa that had an ugly hound trotting in its shade. Not him, either; he looked more like a lumberjack than a fast gun.

That left the man on the roan.

5

Murphy grunted as the third horseman came up in his sights. He was small and slender and he wore his gun low; that *had* to be him. Murphy felt a weakening run through him and he tensed his body against it as though he was clenching a fist. Slowly, very slowly, he lowered the gunsights to the black shirtfront and waited for his target to draw into sure range, then he frowned in surprise as an incongruous sound on that day of heat and dust and imminent death drifted up to him.

It was the sound of music.

Big Hank Brazos had been playing his mouth organ out of key for the past ten miles and now he seemed set to sing out of key for the next ten:

> *Oh, he's a foul-mouthed mule-skinner man,*
> *And he rides with the Ku Klux Klan,*
> *He lives good on fatback, buzzard pie and grits,*
> *Shoots lawmen for fun and throws conniption fits.*

Duke Benedict's nose wrinkled with disgust. "Let me guess—that's your own composition?"

"Well, I'll be dogged, but you're right, Yank." Brazos grinned, his blue eyes wide in his craggy, sun-bronzed face. "How the Sam Hill did you come to guess?"

"Just a wild stab in the dark," the tall and handsome Benedict replied with weary sarcasm. Benedict, who saw himself as a shining example of breeding and refinement, was fully feeling the burden of riding for too long in the company of this overgrown, illiterate Texas brush-popper who played lousy harmonica and composed lousier songs.

Brazos, not quite as innocent as he liked to appear sometimes, winked slyly across at the cowboy who'd joined them at Hondo for the ride up to Spargo. Then he said, "You like my little song, then, Duke?"

The rider in the broadcloth suit and bed-of-flowers vest didn't answer. Benedict knew Brazos and all his tricks. When a trail got long, hot and boring, the big Texan liked nothing better than to try to rile a man. It was his strange way of making the time pass quicker.

"You must be tuckered from the heat, I guess." Brazos smiled at Chad Bowers. "Reckon another verse might cheer him some, Chad?"

Bowers grinned. This hard-faced but easy-going cowboy was still intrigued by his chance trail companions after several hours in their company. The tall gambling man and his massive partner with the purple shirt were hardly the normal run of travelers a man was likely to meet up with in Nevada. And their off-beat appearance was matched by their behavior. Over the long, hot miles, Bowers found himself as fascinated by Duke Benedict's educated dialogue and gentlemanly manners as by Hank Brazos' wild stories and good spirits. He found Brazos' music plenty entertaining; but, sensing Benedict's mounting irritation, elected to leave it up to Brazos to decide if he should sing some more.

Brazos decided he should and filled his lungs:

> *"Oh, he lives in a house on the hill,*
> *And he's got him a squaw named Cripple Creek Jill.*
> *She's happy and greasy and eats vittles for four,*
> *Weighs five hundred pounds and sleeps on the floor."*

Echoes of Brazos' last notes bouncing from the high ridge before them, were suddenly engulfed by the brutal crash of a rifle. Benedict and Brazos saw a puff of smoke atop the ridge, then swung in their saddles as Bowers slid to the ground, his Stetson rolling like a cartwheel down the slope.

Reacting with the blinding speed of a man who had often been a target, Hank Brazos ripped his Winchester from its scabbard with a curse—but he wasn't nearly as quick as Benedict whose twin Peacemakers cut loose at the drygulcher's position in a rolling roar.

Atop the ridge, Murphy clawed dirt frantically as the rider he'd picked as a tinhorn in a fancy vest worked his guns with lightning speed. Snarling lead hornets whined all about him, powdering rock crowns and tearing at the earth.

He'd shot the wrong man. This realization hit Murphy like a kick in the stomach as the Peacemakers continued to belch lead. Only a gunslinger could work guns like that. Damnit, couldn't he do anything right? Then he cursed aloud as a rock fragment split his cheek and suddenly he was frightened. It was time to get to hell and away.

But haste and fear made him careless. As he twisted away from the low, rocky balustrade where he'd waited three hours for his man to show up, he humped his back an inch too high—and Benedict put a slug through his shoulder blade. Murphy, jerked half-erect by the slamming impact of the bullet, screamed in agony. Then the Winchester in Hank Brazos' big hands spewed flame and something went through Murphy's body like a rod of fire.

The ambusher dropped the rifle from nerveless hands and turned slowly on putty legs, his arms crossed over his body as if to stop the lead. But slugs kept coming, spinning him around and sending him over the balustrade. He hit the downslope on his head and went end over end all the way down to the trail.

Slowly the gunsmoke drifted away, mingling with the dust the dry-gulcher had raised on his quick trip down. The rumbling echoes of the guns faded and suddenly the day was emptied of sound.

Hot guns still held at the ready, Hank Brazos and Duke Benedict exchanged grim-faced glances. Veterans of the War Between the States and now saddle-partners in the hunt for one of the deadliest desperadoes ever to steal two hundred thousand dollars in gold bullion, they were no strangers to danger or violent death. Even so, they were shaken by this sudden eruption of violence that had snuffed out two lives in a handful of seconds on a quiet Nevada afternoon.

"You had better check him out," Benedict said finally, inclining his head up-trail. "I'll cover you in case there are any more of the breed skulking about."

Brazos grunted, heeled his appaloosa up to the dead ambusher and swung down.

The dead man was short and red-headed. His ugly face was pocked with the scars of severe acne. His rig was denim, and the old .45 handgun in his belt was rusty. He carried only five dollars on him. Despite his ugliness, he didn't look like a dry-gulcher to Brazos.

Frowning, Brazos climbed the ridge with his dog, Bullpup, to make double-sure the man was alone. He found the ambusher's horse cached in the trees and rode the animal back down to the trail, where Benedict was just finishing going through the things he'd taken from Bowers' pockets.

"Eleven dollars and a letter from his mother in California," Benedict said bitterly as he came erect. "Who the devil would want to kill a man like that? Why?"

Brazos shook his big head. The whole thing seemed pointless, crazy. If he or Benedict had been shot at he would have understood it, what with the enemies they had. But Bowers was just an out-of-work cowpoke, heading up Spargo way hunting work.

10

He sighed and told Benedict about the dry-gulcher. Benedict went along to inspect the corpse while Brazos loaded Bowers' body onto his horse and lashed it in place. Leading Bowers' mount, his own appaloosa and the ambusher's sorrel, he then went up the trail to Benedict who was lighting a cigar and frowning down at the ambusher's corpse.

"What do you make of him, Yank?" Brazos asked.

Benedict shook his head. "Puzzling, Reb. He doesn't appear like the gunman breed. He looks more like a laborer."

"A miner, mebbe?"

Benedict looked at him sharply. "What makes you say that?"

Brazos gestured at the ridge. "His tracks come in from the east. Spargo's east."

"Could be a miner, I suppose. But that still doesn't tell us much, does it?"

"Mebbe it does," Brazos said, his face creased and knotted in thought. "Mebbe this sidewinder wasn't after Bowers. Mebbe he was after us."

"How the devil do you arrive at that conclusion?"

Massive shoulders shrugging under his faded purple shirt, Brazos said, "Well, we don't even know what we're buyin' into in Spargo. Mebbe this feller could—"

"Damnation!" Benedict cut him off. "You're not starting in on that again, are you?" He shook his head. "When you get an idea into that thick skull of yours

11

it takes dynamite to shift it. I suppose you've still got that 'hunch' about Spargo, have you?"

Hank Brazos scowled and folded his arms, sunlight glinting from the mouth organ he wore on a rawhide cord around his neck. He wasn't anxious to resume the argument they'd had in Hondo before pulling out, for Benedict had made him feel a fool then and could doubtless do so again. But he still didn't feel right about this whole deal …

Yesterday in Hondo, Benedict had received a letter from the mining town of Spargo. The two had already spent ten days in Hondo, where the trail of the outlaw they'd been hunting had gone cold, and Foley Kingston had heard they were there. Kingston, who'd served in the Union Army with Benedict, was the biggest man in Spargo from what Brazos could gather. Among other things he was the owner of the silver mine that supported the town. In his letter, Kingston had told Benedict he was in big trouble and needed his help. There was no explanation of the trouble or of what sort of help he needed, and right then and there Brazos had developed his "hunch" that they should turn the request down. Benedict over-rode him, and now here they were, a day's ride from Spargo, and two men were dead. If that didn't back up a man's hunch then Brazos didn't know what did …

He said, "All I'm sayin' is I don't like buyin' into somethin' blind."

"You have already said that," Benedict complained. "Let's ride."

Brazos sighed but didn't argue. He knew he had to stick with Benedict, just the way Benedict had stuck with him throughout their long hunt for Bo Rangle.

Their chase of Bo Rangle dated back to the dying days of the Civil War and a place called Pea Ridge where forces of Confederate and Union troops had fought a bloody battle over a shipment of gold. In the end the gold was snatched away by the infamous Rangle's Raiders. Rebel Sergeant Hank Brazos and Federal Captain Duke Benedict were the sole survivors of one hundred and fifty men. Chance had brought them together at war's end and now they hunted Rangle and the gold brave men had died for. From vastly different backgrounds, Benedict and Brazos disagreed on just about everything under the sun, but their partnership worked, and if Benedict was determined to go on to Spargo, then Brazos had no option but to stick with him, regardless of hunches, dry-gulchers or whatever.

"What are you doing?" Benedict asked as he saw Brazos hefting the dry-gulcher's body across his shoulder.

Brazos dumped the riddled corpse across the sorrel and pulled his lariat from the appaloosa. "Can't leave him here."

"Why not?" Benedict jerked his thumb at Bowers. "Don't tell me he wouldn't have left him to rot."

"It won't hurt us none to take him into Spargo with us," Brazos replied, taking a final pull on the ropes that lashed the dead man to his horse before mounting his appaloosa. "Even dry-gulchers have kin."

"Is that a fact?"

"So I'm told," Brazos murmured and led the way out.

They left the place of death behind and rode with the afternoon sun at their backs. A breeze rose, taking some of the brutal heat out of the day. Birds sang in the trees as they passed and a great mass of billowing white clouds climbed over the Bucksaw Mountains, looking almost too white to be real against the deep blue of the sky.

After a couple of miles, Brazos lifted his mouth organ, blew a few reedy bars in an attempt to cheer himself up, but then he dropped the harmonica and slouched in his saddle, building a smoke.

Benedict nodded understandingly behind him. Most times Benedict didn't want to know what Hank Brazos was thinking, but he believed he knew exactly what the big man's feelings were at that moment. And he was right: Benedict was enjoying the beauty around him and thinking that it was too nice a day to die. Even for a dry-gulcher.

Foley Kingston turned sharply from the liquor cabinet as his wife swept into the huge, chandeliered dining room.

"Well, you finally condescended to come down," he snapped. "I've been holding supper twenty minutes."

"What a gracious greeting, darling," the woman replied, smiling icily, then pirouetting before him to show off her dress. "Do you like this, Foley? It just arrived today from San Francisco."

"How goddamn much does that cost me?"

Ignoring the question, Rhea Kingston turned her back on her husband to admire her reflection in the long wall mirror beneath the Du Lesse mural. The first lady of Spargo looked even more beautiful than usual tonight and she knew it. Taller than average and built on the long, slender lines of a thorough-bred, she was sheathed in a floor-length, clinging creation of finest white taffeta, cut daringly low to reveal the sculptured perfection of her magnificent breasts. Her rich auburn hair was piled high and long diamond ear-rings dangled from aristocratic ears. She executed the cruel, knowing smile of a woman sure of her power when she saw Kingston's expression change from anger to desire in the mirror.

"My chair, Foley," she said, turning to the table.

Resentment brought a flush of blood to Kingston's face. He didn't mind holding a chair for a woman but he hated being ordered to. "We don't have any god-damn company tonight," he growled. Then, "Ring for the servants if you want somebody to pull your chair out."

Slanted green eyes glittered and the deeply cleft bosom lifted. "My chair, Foley."

Foley Kingston didn't give in ... not right away. The owner of Spargo's Motherlode Mine was the most powerful man in a hundred miles and hadn't grown used to being bossed by a woman, even after two stormy years of marriage. His first wife had never tried it, but then she hadn't been anything like Rhea.

He was able to stand his ground until he made the mistake of lifting his gaze from the array of expensive silver and china to her face. Immediately his stubbornness and determination dissolved. She was irresistibly beautiful. Cursing his weakness, he pulled out her chair. As she seated herself he kissed her naked shoulder. She flinched.

"Really, Foley, don't you think it's much too hot for that sort of thing?"

"Hot?" Kingston snapped, angry and embarrassed as he went to his chair and sat down hard. "I don't think it's the heat we have to worry about in this house, Rhea. Every time I touch you lately it seems you freeze up like Christmas in—"

"Please, darling, I'm not in the mood to hear about my shortcomings in bed this evening."

The mouth of the tall, iron-faced man became a steel trap as he pushed himself halfway out of his chair.

"By God, Rhea, sometimes you talk like a whore—damned if you don't."

"I'll have turtle," she said.

Kingston's eyes bugged. "What?" Then he noticed that Pancho the Mexican houseboy had come in, soundlessly as always. Rhea was ordering soup.

"By glory, someday I'll maim you for creeping up on me like that, wetback!" he snarled, turning his fury on the less formidable target.

"Oh, let the man be, Foley," Rhea said, bored. "There is no need to take it out on the servants just because your gunfighter hasn't arrived."

"I am not worried, and Duke Benedict is not a gunfighter."

She smiled mockingly. "Oh, no, that's right, he is a former comrade-in-arms and man of distinction, isn't he?"

"As a matter of fact, he is very much a man of distinction."

"I'm sure. That is why you sent for him, isn't it, because he is a gentleman? And of course you didn't really mean it when you spread the word around that he was the important somebody who, to quote you, 'will put all the dirty Cousin Jacks back in their places?' Really, Foley, sometimes I believe you grow so devious that you confuse yourself."

"I didn't spread that story at all. I don't know how it got started. But I do know that—"

"We'll both have turtle soup," Rhea said to Pancho. "And what will you have for the main course, darling, mutton or veal?"

17

"You really don't give a damn, do you?" Kingston said. "You don't care that my mine is idle or that those ignorant Irish micks won't go back to work until I agree to spend thousands of dollars re-timbering the shafts. You don't care that everything I've built up here is suddenly in jeopardy, do you?"

"Mutton, Pancho," she said, "for both of us."

Kingston bit his lip in fury as the Mexican vanished. A tense silence fell over the room. Rhea turned her head from side to side, watching her reflection in the big windows that commanded a panoramic view of the mining town spread below Kingston Hill. Toying with his soup, Kingston watched his wife from under lowered brows, wishing he could hate her but doubting that he could.

He was relieved when his son Cole came in to tell him that Art Shadie wanted to see him. Cole, Kingston's son from his first marriage, was a tall, well-made man of twenty-two with an open, guileless face. In the years between the death of his first wife and his marriage to Rhea, Foley had been close to his son, but they'd drifted apart shortly after Rhea came to the house. It was clear that his wife and his son barely tolerated each other, and he suspected that this was Rhea's fault.

"Tell Shadie he can come in, Cole," Kingston said.

"Really, Foley," Rhea admonished as Cole went out, "there's no earthly reason why you can't talk with

18

Shadie after the meal. Your precious mine isn't going to cave in during the next half hour is it?"

"It's not the mine I'm concerned about tonight."

She looked at him closely. "Where has Shadie been the past few days, Foley?"

"Down south," was all he would say, and he was rewarded by the curiosity she wasn't able to conceal as Shadie shuffled in, hat in hand.

"Evenin', boss, Mrs. Kingston."

Art Shadie was the boss of the ten-man crew of hard-cases that were known around Spargo as Kingston's Regulators. He was a tough, blocky, broken-nosed gun-toter with greasy black hair and a disconcerting habit of wiping his nose with his sleeve. Kingston regarded him as a rough diamond but a trusted and valuable employee. Rhea considered him a pig.

"Well?" Kingston said.

Shadie glanced uncertainly at Rhea.

"Let's have just the nugget of it, Shadie," Kingston said. "Was your journey south successful or otherwise?"

Shadie grinned. "Successful, boss. I, er, seen that joker and he reckons he can handle your little prob-lem, no trouble at—"

"Use your kerchief, Mr. Shadie," Rhea said icily.

Shadie broke off, jaw hanging open. He flushed when he realized he'd been unconsciously lifting his sleeve to his face as he talked. A tough, sometimes dangerous man, Shadie felt and acted like a school-boy in Rhea Kingston's disturbing presence.

"Leave the man be, Rhea," Kingston said, touching a table napkin to his lips and looking unusually pleased with himself. Then, to Shadie, "Money side right, too?"

Still red-faced, Shadie nodded. "Reckon so, boss."

"Fine, fine. Well, you've done well, Shadie, very well. We'll discuss things in greater detail later. In the meantime, have yourself a good bath and a meal; you've earned it."

"Right, boss." Shadie nodded to Rhea as he turned to go and she saw the look of hunger in the man's eyes, despite the fact that she'd gone out of her way to belittle him. She was accustomed to adulation from men wherever she went, and she was amused by Shadie's interest.

Shadie paused at the door. "Er, you plan on goin' out tonight, boss? The boys want to know if you'll need 'em." Since the mine had closed, Kingston hadn't felt free to venture abroad at night without protection.

"No," Kingston said. "Mrs. Kingston and I are having a quiet evening at home together."

"How utterly charming," Rhea said as Shadie closed the door behind him.

"It might be a good thing if you refrained from sarcasm in front of the help," Kingston said critically, but he was unable to conceal how pleased he was by Shadie's news.

Rhea was openly curious. "What is going on, Foley? What are you up to?"

"I'm not sure I understand, my dear."

"Why did Shadie go south?"

"Just business. It would only bore you if I told you. Business matters always do, don't they, darling?"

"It's something to do with the strike, isn't it? And it's somehow connected with this Benedict person, isn't it?"

The quick, sharp look that crossed his face told Rhea that she'd hit the target, but his reply was bland:

"A strange assumption, Rhea. More greens?"

She leaned on her elbows, her face lovely in the soft light, her green eyes intense. "Why are you bringing Duke Benedict here, Foley? I mean the *real* reason? You say you need him to help you in your trouble with the miners, but Shadie and the others seem quite capable of handling things. Why do you feel you need Benedict? Could it be that you're expecting things to get much worse?"

As had happened many times, Foley Kingston found himself impressed by his wife's hard-edged intelligence. He smiled and said, "Let us say that it is my little secret for the time being. I enjoy my secrets, my dear, just as you enjoy yours."

"What is that supposed to mean?"

Kingston bit his lip. He hadn't meant to say that.

"Speak up, Foley. You're never short of a few thousand words. What is my secret supposed to be?"

Kingston's face had turned almost haggard, but nothing could have made him reveal what he'd hinted at. After all, he wasn't certain if his wife was being unfaithful to him. And if she was, he didn't really want to know.

TWO

TWO FOR SPARGO

Old Billy Murphy poked left and right with his crutch to clear a path for himself through the funeral parlor doorway.

"Out of me way, damn and bedevil you! Is it true what I'm hearin'?"

The miners cleared a path for him. Like Murphy, most of them were Irish. Their grim looks answered his questions more eloquently than words and for a moment the fierce-faced old man seemed drained of the power to move or speak as he stood leaning on his crutch staring from face to face.

Then undertaker Bert Egstrom, long, gaunt and solemn, appeared in the doorway leading to the bigger room where he kept the coffins. Egstrom rubbed his dry hands together and said, "He's in here, Mr. Murphy."

Murphy swung around. There were a dozen or so men in the second room where three pinewood coffins stood on carpenter's horses. The shades were drawn against the glare of the sun, but the room was gloomy rather than cool. Two strangers stood leaning against the bench along the far wall. On the bench behind them with a pair of boots sticking out was a canvas-covered shape. In the center of the room an uncovered body lay on another heavy bench. The body had red hair, the color Old Billy Murphy's had been before it turned pure white.

Murphy's lips twitched as he moved to the bench to stare down at his son. His sick drinker's face paled, making the network of red veins stand out. On one cheek was a big mole like a peg driven into the skin.

"Murdered!" he whispered in the thick quiet, his eyes taking in the ugly holes studding the corpse. "Look how they murdered me son!"

"You have my deepest sympathy, Mr. Murphy," Egstrom murmured with professional gloom. "We all understand how you must feel."

"The devil you do!" blazed the old man whose temper could be impressive even if he was as skinny as a snake and half crazy. His red-rimmed eyes bulged as he jabbed a shaking finger at the corpse. "Look at him in the name of St. Patrick—massacred he is! What did they slaughter me darlin' boy with, a Gatlin' gun? Who did it? What blackguard committed the foul deed? Tell me, God rot your souls!"

The miners looked silently at the two strangers. Old Billy Murphy straightened slowly as he stared at them, a giant in a faded purple shirt and a tall man dressed like a gambler. His eyes flicked down to the low-hung guns they wore, then lifted again to their faces. Their expressions were devoid of either sympathy or guilt as they met the terrible accusation of his glare.

"*They* are the murderers?" His voice was a hoarse whisper.

Bert Egstrom made to explain, but Duke Benedict cut him off. "We shot your son, Murphy. He ambushed us yesterday afternoon along the Hondo Trail."

"Liar!" the old man screamed. "Tommy was a good boy, a gentle, clean-livin'—"

"Save it, joker," Brazos said. "We've been talkin' to folks about your son. Seems he was a rotten-tempered little polecat that's been in trouble all his life."

Murphy tried to speak but rage choked him off.

"We also have a fair idea what he was up to," put in Benedict, who had coaxed considerable information about Tommy Murphy from the gabby Egstrom before the old man arrived. "As you might have guessed by now, my name is Benedict. I'm a friend of—"

"Benedict!" Murphy gasped. "Kingston's hired gun!"

"Kingston's friend," corrected Benedict who'd been puzzled to learn earlier that not only was his arrival anticipated in the mining town, but he was reputed to be a gun-for-hire whom Foley Kingston had imported. "I'm not a hired gun, even though it seems many of you believe so." He pointed to the corpse of Tommy Murphy. "He believed it, old man, and it is my educated guess that he rode out yesterday to try and account for me before I could get to Spargo. Would that be right, old man?"

"Lies!" Murphy gasped. He stared in mute appeal at the men about him, but their eyes fell away from his glance. They were big, rough, muscular men, mostly illiterate and violent and suspicious by nature, but they shared a respect bordering on dread of men of the fast gun breed. Well before Benedict's arrival in Spargo, his name had been bruited about as a wonder gunman and bloody-handed killer. His arrival with big Brazos and two dead men across their saddles, backed by his air of authority and the double guns he wore, seemed to support all they'd heard about him.

Old Billy Murphy sensed their reluctance to support him and it enraged him even more. Swinging away from his son's body, he advanced towards Benedict and Brazos with words spilling out of him as if they scalded his mouth.

"Hired killers! The lowest breed there is! You don't have loyalty to any man—just to the dirty dollar." He halted before them, gesticulating. "You come to a town where honest, God-fearin' and hard-workin' men are locked in an honest fight for better conditions with a money-grubbin' rich man—and you kill a man's son and then flaunt his death as if it was somethin' noble you'd done." The old man's body shook with the force of his emotion, and he lifted his crutch as if to lash out with it. "Killers! Well, I'm not afeared of you even if everybody else seems to be. I won't be backin' and crawlin' and—"

His tirade was interrupted by a menacing growl. The old man jumped back, nearly falling as Bullpup scurried from behind the two men and bared his teeth at the threatening crutch.

"Mother of God!" the old man yelped. "What in the name of Lucifer is it?"

Pleased by the effect his appearance created, the massive, bull-headed hound barked to identify himself as a dog, then squatted when Brazos snapped his fingers at him.

"Like me, he don't take kindly to pilgrims bellerin' and shoutin'," Brazos said. Murphy, recovering from his shock, started to talk again, but Brazos overrode him. "Look, old feller, you don't seem to get the straight of this. Instead of you roarin' and dirty-namin' us, you ought to be grateful we brought your dry-gulchin' son in with us instead of leavin' him—"

"Dry-gulchin'?" Murphy cried. "What foulness is this? Who are ye sayin' me boy killed?"

"Him." Benedict flicked the canvas cover from the second corpse. "Chad Bowers, old man, an

27

out-of-work cowboy who joined us to ride up here looking for honest work—shot down like a dog by your fine son. Now what do you have to say?"

Murphy swallowed convulsively as he stared down at Bowers' waxen face, then he turned away. "I'm not believin' it," he panted, but he didn't sound convincing. "Me boy wouldn't do a man in that way."

"You reckon not?" Brazos said. "Well, tell us this, mister. If your boy wasn't out huntin' trouble, what was he doin' twenty miles along the Hondo Trail? Mebbe you can explain that on account nobody else seems to have much idea."

For a moment a trapped, furtive look crossed Murphy's face. Then he grew defiant. "All right, all right, spout your filthy lies in a bereaved old man's face—spit on a father's grief if you will ... but there'll be a reckonin' for ye, by all the saints there will be!"

He gestured contemptuously at the men who'd been watching the clash in tense silence.

"Everybody on our side of the fence in this unlucky town isn't old like me or yellow-gutted like them here that calls themselves men. Just wait until Clancy hears about this, you butchers, then you'll be smirkin' on the other side of your faces. Clancy'll be knowin' how to deal with your dirty breed—and don't you be makin' no mistake about that."

Benedict and Brazos exchanged exasperated glances, nodded, and without a word headed for the door together. Suddenly they'd had enough of

28

the smell of death and Old Billy Murphy's mouth. Suddenly they needed air.

"Clancy!" the old man's shout followed them out. "He'll see you rue the day you come to do Kingston's bloody work for him."

Benedict halted when they hit the street, tugging out a cigar and frowning back at the funeral parlor. "Just as well we left when we did," he said tightly. "I was about up to here with that old fool calling me a paid killer."

Brazos' gaze played over the dusty street as he stood with his weight on one leg, hip thrust out, and twisting a smoke. "Seems he ain't the only one hereabout with that idea, Yank. Seems the whole damned town figures it the same way." He licked his cigarette into shape, set it between his teeth. "How come, you reckon?"

Exhaling a cloud of blue cigar smoke, Benedict shook his head as they moved slowly off along the shady side of the street. "I don't rightly know, Reb," he said thoughtfully. "For one, I'm not a gunfighter, and even if I were, I can't understand why Foley Kingston should put out a story like that."

Brazos lifted his gaze to the mansion that stood atop the steep, round-crowned hill at the far end of Spargo's main stem, Johnny Street. Spargo, a poor-man town of frame, adobe and tarpaper, was set on white alkali flats, half encircled on the eastern side by the Bucksaw Mountains. Spargo's dust, heat and almost palpable stink of poverty made Foley Kingston's mansion that much more impressive by comparison.

It was a big, white two-storied house with lofty marble colonnades and rows of glittering colonial windows now reflecting the yellow sun. Surrounded by heavy shade trees and high iron fences, the building reminded Brazos powerfully of the great serene plantation mansions of the South that he'd fought to defend during the war—before Benedict's bunch got busy burning them to the ground. The similarity seemed all the stronger because of the contrast between the opulence and the poverty, just as it had been in Georgia and Tennessee.

Brazos said, "Just what sort of a feller is this Kingston, Benedict?"

"What sort? Well, he's an officer and a gentleman for starters."

Brazos was unimpressed. "If all the sons-of-bitches I've ever struck that called theirselves officers and gentlemen was laid out end-to-end, it'd likely be a good thing. I mean what's he *really* like?"

"You'll soon find out for yourself. We're going up to see him as soon as we've checked into the hotel and spruced up."

"Mebbe we should've gone to see him afore we took them bodies to the undertaker's."

"No ... no, I wanted to get the feel of this place before I saw Foley."

"Do you reckon you got the feel of it yet?"

Benedict wasn't sure. Certainly they'd already learned a great deal about Spargo. The town was locked in a strike between the miners and Foley Kingston. The miners, claiming that the Motherlode Mine was unsafe following a series of fatal accidents, were refusing to work until conditions were improved. According to Egstrom, the undertaker, the trouble, six weeks old now with no sign of capitulation on either side, had been marked by frequent violent clashes between the strikers and Kingston's men.

Obviously a desperate situation, Benedict thought. As for getting the feel of the place, he didn't know about that. There was something about Spargo that couldn't be absorbed in a hurry, he reflected as he met the scowling stares of a group of denim-jacketed men loafing in the arcade on the central block. The taste and smell of Spargo was not merely of its dust, which seemed to hang above it in an eternal pall, but it was the taste of suspicion and the smell of fear and anger.

"Perhaps the funeral parlor is not the ideal place to get the feel of a town," Benedict suggested, halting opposite a lofty building where the batwings stood propped open to catch any whiff of breeze. He smiled for the first time since they rode over the bridge across Cherry Creek with the dead men. "If you get my meaning?"

Brazos peered across at the sign that read:

> SILVER KING SALOON
> ACE BEAUFORD PROP.
> BEER! WHISKY! GIRLS!

Not being able to read or write, the sign could have been written in Arabic for all Brazos knew, but he'd never needed book-learning to be able to recognize a saloon. His grin answering Benedict's, he pushed his battered disaster of a hat to the back of his big head, spat on his hands with the air of a man about to undertake a pleasurable job of work and led the way across the street … totally unaware of the eyes of the most dangerous man in Spargo drilling at them from the Chisum Street corner.

Clancy was his name and ruling the Spargo roost was his game. As wild a son as Mother Ireland had produced in many a long and hungry generation, he stood six feet four from his brass-heeled boots to the top of his great curly head. He dressed out at two hundred and fifty pounds of bone and muscle and fiery temperament and was the swaggering, bullying, blarneying boss of Spargo's army of Irish miners. Sly and violent, crafty and hot-headed, he was the leader not because he was most gifted to lead, but because his iron fists had long since hammered down the last man who'd sought to contest his place at the top of the heap. Afraid of only one living person, a skinny little old woman he called mother, it was Clancy who'd brought the Spargo miners out on strike, and now he was committed to keeping them out, every ugly one of them, until Foley Kingston had given in to their demands. This was Patrick Michael Clancy. Himself.

"Which one is Benedict?" he asked in a peat-bog brogue to runty little Larry O'Rourke who stood with him on the corner watching the two tall men crossing Johnny Street for the Silver King. "The gombeen in the tinhorn suit or the great lump with the hound?"

"The one in the suit, Paddy," supplied O'Rourke, who had gone to fetch Clancy when the two strangers had arrived at Egstrom's with the dead men. "Didn't I tell you he looked a bad one and all? You see the two guns he's got hangin' off his belt?"

"I see 'em, right enough." Clancy smacked his palm with a giant fist. "I see 'em …"

O'Rourke waited patiently for some ten seconds, then looked up expectantly. "Well, what are you waitin' for, Clancy? Are you goin' to be bustin' his head in for him before he can slaughter any more brave boys?"

To O'Rourke's surprise, Paddy Clancy shook his curly head slowly and deliberately as he stared at the doors the two men had vanished through. O'Rourke, a weasel-faced little man who played parasite pilot fish to Clancy's shark, said innocently:

"Surely you're not for lettin' the man get away with the foul murder of poor Murphy now, Clancy?"

"'Tweren't murder."

O'Rourke's jaw fell open. "It weren't?"

"The young idjut was for listenin' too much to his old man," Clancy explained. "Old Billy reckoned we oughta try and stop this Benedict before he got here, and Tommy, wantin' to make a big man of himself, begged me to let him try."

"And so you did, eh?"

"To be sure ... but I should have known better. Young Murphy was nivver much smarter than Old Billy ... and his brain is addled by hate and whisky. He wanted to be a hero and all he done was kill a cowboy and make an ugly corpse of himself."

O'Rourke's skinny shoulders slumped and he pulled out a kerchief and coughed into it. He wasn't much surprised to hear the truth about Murphy; he'd always found him a poisonous little echo of his mad old man at best. But he was disappointed that Clancy wasn't about to avenge Murphy's death. Sickly, plagued by a hacking cough, unemployable, and not too long for this world, one of the few pleasures O'Rourke had left was tagging after Clancy and enjoying the violence that followed the giant like a shadow.

"So ... so you're just goin' to forget the whole terrible business, are ye, Clancy?" he said, making one last try.

"I'm not goin' to go jumpin' a man they're sayin' handles guns like me mother handles a set of rosary beads," Clancy growled. "But I'm not goin' to forget it neither."

He hitched at his broad leather belt. "The high-steppin' tenderfoot'll bleed for what he's done, make no mistake," he concluded, and then he swaggered down the street to pay his last respects to Tommy Murphy. After that he'd confer long and earnestly with his secret partner, a man of money and power and sinister ambition who saw in Benedict's arrival a threatening new element introduced into the life-or-death game they were playing with Foley Kingston.

THREE

AT THE MOTHERLODE

Hank Brazos was bored.

Seated uncomfortably on an expensive-looking settee that he wasn't any too sure would support his weight, he'd smoked a cigarette through the hearty reunion of old comrades-in-arms, puffed silently through another as glorious deeds in the Union Army were relived, and had finished a tasteless third by the time Benedict told Kingston about their clash with the dry-gulcher and Kingston discussed his stalemate with the miners.

Now they were back to "glorious deeds" again.

Brazos scratched his navel, fiddled with his harmonica, then squinted out the big windows at Bullpup sprawled in the window light on the gallery. He wondered if he could take another cigarette.

The settee creaked alarmingly as he shifted his weight and scowled across the room at the two men standing before the cold hearth. He scowled anew as they matched fancy accents and used unpronounceable words, half of which he was sure they were making up as they went along.

He tried to be objective. Would he be less bored if Benedict and Kingston weren't boasting about how they'd knocked the blue-eyed bejasus out of the Johnny Rebs with whom he, ex-Sergeant Hank Brazos, had served for four years? Would he be any more interested if they'd been on his side and were reliving heroic days of booting Yank backsides through Georgia instead of the other way around?

He doubted it. What really bothered him were the big words and the fine manners that back in Texas would be considered unmanly. He'd been riding with Benedict long enough to understand that this sort of carry-on was normal amongst the rich and the educated, but that didn't help much. Benedict alone he'd learned to put up with, but two of the same breed together in one room hacking over the war from the Yank side of the fence, well, that was a little rich for his blood.

"Another drink, Hank?"

Suddenly he realized that Kingston was speaking to him. The interruption gave him a reason to get up from the settee which was threatening to cave in beneath him.

"Not right now," he drawled, rolling his shoulders to take the stiffness out of them.

"Duke? You'll have another?"

"A small one, Foley."

Brazos' scowl returned as he watched Kingston pour. He was dry enough, but he didn't like what was being offered. Scotch, Kingston called it. Said it was whisky. Perhaps it was, but it sure wasn't rye or bourbon or sourmash or any whisky he'd tasted before. He wondered if he ought to ask Kingston for a beer for Bullpup whose tongue was hanging out a foot. He decided against it as he moved across the room to lean against the wall by the windows and tug out his Bull Durham to roll a cigarette he didn't really want. He could imagine Mr. Bigtime Kingston lifting his eyebrows and saying, "Beer? *What* is beer?"

Benedict and Kingston were talking about the miners again when the double oak doors opened and Cole Kingston returned to the room. Kingston had sent the young man out ten minutes before to bring Mrs. Kingston down to meet them. Kingston broke off with a frown when he saw that his son was alone.

"Where is Mrs. Kingston, Cole?"

"She said she's not feeling well, Dad," Cole replied, and even Brazos could tell he wasn't speaking the truth.

"Nonsense," Kingston said, "she's the healthiest woman in Nevada." He frowned. "You told her Mr. Benedict was here, didn't you?"

"Sure, Dad."

"What did she say?"

Cole looked uncomfortably at Benedict. "Rhea's not in the best of moods today, Dad. Maybe I shouldn't—"

"I want to know why she refuses to come down," Kingston snapped. "What did she say to you?"

"Well … well, she said she … she had no interest in meeting paid killers. Sorry, Mr. Benedict."

The room went quiet.

Foley Kingston banged down his glass. "Oh, she did, did she? Well, we'll see about that."

"Just a moment, Foley," Benedict said as Kingston made for the door. "I can meet Mrs. Kingston another time, but what she said raises a point I'd like to clear up."

Sensing what Benedict meant, Brazos found he wasn't bored any more as Kingston turned slowly back to the room and said quietly, "And what's that, Duke?"

His thumbs hooked into the arm-holes of the bed-of-flowers vest that he'd put on over a tailored white silk shirt after his bath at the Spargo Hotel, Benedict replied, "Your wife has referred to me as a paid killer, Foley. Down at the funeral parlor, I had the same epithet directed at me more than once." A frown creased his dark brows. "I don't understand this. My profession, if I have one at present, is gambling. I've never hired my gun and never will … something I believe you know. How did this story about me being a hired gun get started?"

Foley Kingston's hard, handsome face broke into an apologetic grin. "I'm afraid I'm to blame for that, Duke."

"I don't understand."

Kingston spread his hands, his gaze embracing Brazos as well as Benedict. "It's a simple matter of distortion. Duke, when I heard you were in Hondo, I sent for you because I was in dire trouble and because I remembered you from the war as the best hand with a gun I'd ever seen. When I received your letter telling me you could come, I must admit that, to put a dampener on the spirits of my enemies here, I let it be known that a very formidable friend of mine was coming to Spargo to help protect my interests. And that was all I said, Duke, no more. But the miners in their ignorant, Irish way decided you were a notorious hired gun, and once the story got started there was no stopping it."

"I see," Benedict murmured. "But your wife, Foley? She seems to believe it, too."

"Women, Duke," Kingston said ruefully. "As I remember, you were something of an expert on the species. Who knows how or why they get anything into their heads?"

Smiling, Benedict nodded in acceptance of the explanation, then glanced at the big ornate clock over the mantel. "Well, I guess we'll be going, Foley.

It's been something of an eventful day, and another is undoubtedly coming up tomorrow."

"Eventful and I trust, peaceful, Duke."

Realizing that he must have missed out on something said earlier, Brazos pushed himself off the wall as Benedict picked up his low-crowned black hat from a table.

"What's on tomorrow, Yank?"

"Didn't you hear us discussing it?" Benedict replied. "Foley wants me to help him gain access to his—"

"Gain what?" Brazos' brow looked like a corrugated iron roof.

"Get into," Benedict explained patiently. "Three weeks ago, the miners took over the Motherlode Mine to force Foley into meeting their demands. You'll recall we saw a lot of miners loafing about the mine gate on our way in; well, they're there to prevent Foley or his men getting to the mine for any reason. Obviously this can't go on, and tomorrow, with my help, Foley intends to go in."

Barrel chest gleaming in the lamplight through the gap in his unbuttoned purple shirt, Brazos scratched his neck and looked at Kingston. "Locked you outa your own mine? Sounds kinda illegal to me."

"A lot that has happened here over the past months is illegal and worse, Hank," Kingston declared. Then, with a thoughtful expression as his eyes played over Brazos' Herculean physique, he added, "Will you be riding with us tomorrow, Hank? Duke introduced you as his trail partner but he didn't make it clear if you would be assisting him."

Benedict looked at Brazos. He hadn't committed him because that wasn't the way their partnership worked. They'd joined forces to hunt Bo Rangle and two hundred thousand in Confederate gold, nothing else. Whatever cropped up along the way was judged on its merits; there was no obligation for one to support the other if he didn't want to.

Brazos knew the decision was up to him. If Benedict weren't involved, he would most likely stay out of it. From what he could figure out, the trouble in Spargo was a conflict between one-eyed Kingston and a stubborn bunch of miners. There were probably faults aplenty on both sides.

But Benedict *was* involved, and because it could well be a dangerous situation at the Motherlode Mine when Kingston tried to force his way in tomorrow, Brazos declared that he would go along.

"I'm in," Brazos said.

"Why, I certainly appreciate this, Hank," Kingston beamed, patting him on the shoulder. "He's got the look of a fighter or I'm no judge, eh, Duke?"

"He makes out," was all Benedict was prepared to say.

The gambling man looked preoccupied as Foley and Cole Kingston showed them out, but it wasn't until he spotted Art Shadie and a couple of Kingston's "Regulators" loafing in the moon shadow at the far end of the long, pillared gallery that he was prompted to put into words something that had been puzzling him throughout the evening with Kingston.

"Foley," he said, fitting his hat to his head at exactly the right angle, "it seems to me that you aren't exactly short of trouble-shooters without Brazos and me."

"Good boys," Kingston said, inclining his head at the men, "and capable enough, but in a limited way. They've been able to look after things so far, but I wouldn't have faith in them if things really got out of hand, you understand? They are tough and reliable, but they don't have the brains and the class you have, Duke."

"You're expecting things to get worse'n they are now?" said Brazos, squatting down to scratch Bullpup's ears as the dog came swaggering up to him.

"Let us say I believe in preparedness," Kingston replied. "Now, Duke, are you sure you wish to stay at the hotel? I can put you up here with no trouble at all."

Benedict declined the offer, explaining that they'd already booked into the Spargo House Hotel.

"Well, as you wish." Kingston smiled. "Until tomorrow, gentlemen."

Their boots crunched on the gravel drive as they headed for the big gates. They were silent, each occupied with his own thoughts as they passed through the gates and trod the broad trail that led to town. The night was still hot under a brilliant moon that washed the Bucksaws to the east in silver and fell upon the rooftops of Spargo. Even at night, the eternal dust fogged around the town, blurring its edges. But the dust didn't seem to reach up here. It was a different world on Kingston Hill.

They'd travelled a hundred yards or so, walking in black pools of moon shadow, before Benedict glanced at the ox-shouldered figure beside him and realized Brazos was wearing his thoughtful look.

"Something on your mind?" Benedict asked.

"Could be."

"Spill it then."

"I'm thinkin' about tomorrow."

"What about it?"

"Could be kinda hairy."

"Almost bound to be. But what about it?"

"You say you owe Kingston, Yank?"

"Yes. He saved my life at the first battle of Bull Run."

"And you elected to come here to cancel out the debt?"

"That's so. But I still don't get what you're driving at."

"Then I'll put it plain. Would you be ready to work for Kingston here if you never owed him?"

Benedict smiled knowingly. "You don't like Foley. I thought I could read the signs."

"It's surprisin' how few dudes who talk like furriners and get around makin' out they're better'n everybody else I do like, Benedict."

"Never mind the heavy-footed sarcasm. You don't like Kingston, do you?"

"That ain't important, is it? I just come along for the pony ride here. What signifies is what you think of him now you've seen him again after a few years."

"You're asking me has he changed?" Benedict asked and Brazos nodded. "Well, as a matter of fact, he has. I enjoyed seeing him again and going over old times—"

"Like how you two whupped Robert E. Lee all by yourselves?"

"Yes, like that. But those days seemed very long ago, talking with Foley tonight. He's become … well, somewhat hard and calculating." Benedict paused to watch a night bird sweep above them and then added, almost to himself, "Perhaps ruthless as well …"

"In other words, you don't like him much either?"

"You're saying that, not me." Benedict's voice was testy now. "In any case, what's the purpose of all this talk? Make your point if you have one."

Brazos halted, hands on hips. "Okay, I will. The truth of it is, Yank, I don't much like the set-up in this man's town. The way I see it, you got a bunch of woolly headed miners bellyachin' about their no-good boss on one hand, and on the other you got a hard-headed jasper like Kingston bellyachin' about his no-good miners. The miners are bound and determined not to work the mine again until Kingston makes it safe, and Kingston ain't going to back down to no bunch of miners no matter what." He spread his hands. "Standoff. So who's right and who's wrong?"

"Well, the answer to that is probably neither and both."

"Well, there you go … it ain't fittin' to buy in on a ruckus where you don't know who's in the right."

"Kingston's right."

"But you just said—"

"I owe Kingston," Benedict snapped, moving off. "I owe him and this is my chance to cancel out an obligation. That makes him right."

Brazos opened his mouth to argue but nothing came out, for, staring at Benedict's tall, receding figure, he realized that he'd look on the whole thing just as Benedict did if he was in his boots. When you owed a man he had to be right, at least until you squared the account. It was part of the Code, and in the West the Code meant more to a man than the Bible. Or his life …

"Here they come!"

The warning rippled through the ranks of the miners assembled before the gates of the Motherlode Mine. Eyes tightening, empty, work-roughened hands clenched into fists, they turned their heads to face the riders swinging into sight around the towering bulk of Clinton's barn.

"Where's the rest of 'em?" Larry O'Rourke said as he counted the horsemen and looked in vain for more in the hoof-kicked dust beyond them. "There's only three of 'em."

"Likely that's all that Foley Kingston believes he needs," Brian Hoolihan said. "That's his two new guns he's bringin' in with him. Benedict and Brazos."

"By glory he'll be findin' out he's needin' more than jist them two murderin' divils to get through these gates," declared Old Billy Murphy. Leaning on his crutch by the closed gates, Murphy was still in the dark suit he'd worn to his son's funeral earlier that morning. The defiant words that came from his shrunken mouth seemed strangely at odds with his feeble, crippled body, but there was determination enough in his blazing eyes … and more than a hint of madness.

"Now just be takin' it easy, Billy," said the quiet voice of Shamus Delaney. "We won't gain a thing today by getting over-excited."

Old Billy glared defiance at the speaker. Stoop shouldered Delaney stood with a handful of men Paddy Clancy had dubbed "the Shakies" because they refused to support some of the hard-line measures in the strike he'd called. Delaney had once held a lot of influence in Spargo, but it had dwindled sharply since Clancy seized the reins.

"Take it easy while me darlin' boy is molderin' in his grave, Delaney?" shouted Billy Murphy. "Is that what you're wantin'?"

"Shut your loud old mouth!"

Murphy whirled angrily, then wilted and fell petulantly silent when he realized it was Clancy himself who'd spoken. The biggest man in the bunch by almost a full head, Clancy was standing with O'Rourke at the rear of the group by the fence. Bareheaded in the blazing sun, with his thick mane of curls gleaming like beaten bronze, Clancy looked sober and grim.

A snort of disgust shook Murphy. It seemed they were all jumpy but him. He was damned if he could understand why Clancy had forbidden any of them to bring guns along. Clancy had said that Kingston would have no excuse for introducing gunplay if they were unarmed. Murphy thought that was crazy. There were thirty of them here today. If they'd brought guns, they'd be a hell of a lot more than a match for Benedict and Brazos.

When the riders were less than fifty yards away, a hot breeze came up and sent dust snatching at the skirt of a woman further down the street as she hurried to her house and went inside, closing the door behind her.

Foley Kingston rode in the lead on his white thoroughbred stallion. Duke Benedict was a little behind and to Kingston's left. The wind ruffled the sleeves of his white shirt and tugged at the four-in-hand tie. From the shadow of his low-crowned hat, clear gray eyes took in the men. Bullpup preceded Hank Brazos on his spotted appaloosa to Kingston's right.

Even though the horse was a barrel-chested eighteen hands, its rider looked almost too big for it.

Another ten yards and then Clancy's voice sounded, sudden and loud:

"That's far enough, Kingston!"

The horsemen kept coming. The miners shuffled uneasily, looking over their shoulders at Clancy. Clancy waited a handful of seconds, then said, "All right, lads, turn them around."

The miners surged forward. Kingston checked his horse and Benedict and Brazos drew abreast and reined in. Nobody saw Benedict draw, but suddenly one of his big Colts was angled at the miners. There was a milling moment of uncertainty, then they came to a halt with ten feet separating them from the naked gun.

"So it's guns and bullets against flesh and blood and empty hands, is it?" Paddy Clancy shouted contemptuously. "I suppose this is what you call a fair shake, Kingston, you yellow-livered cur!"

"That's tellin' 'im, Clancy lad!" shrieked Old Billy Murphy, his red-veined face flushed with excitement. He shook a trembling fist. "We're not afraid of your dirty hired guns, Kingston! You'll have to kill us to get through here!"

"You're acting like fools," Kingston said calmly. "You have been doing that all along, but I've finally reached the end of my patience." He pointed over their heads at the mine gates. "That is my personal property in there and I don't intend to permit you riff-raff to—"

"Riff-raff?" echoed a thick-muscled miner with a snarl. "By Judas, boys, are we goin' to stand for that?"

"You'll stand for it, mister," Benedict said softly, moving the gun to cover the man. "You will also stand aside. Mr. Kingston is coming through."

Indecision flickered in the miners' eyes as they stared up at the expressionless face behind the gun. There was no telling if Benedict was bluffing or not. He might be, but they couldn't be sure.

A touch of spur sent Benedict's horse forward. "Come on, move aside!"

The miners went back a step, then stood fast at a word from Clancy. Forced to rein in, Benedict cocked his Colt but still they wouldn't open up.

Then suddenly Brazos was out of his saddle and approaching the miners with an easy grin on his battle-scarred face. "Back off, boys. You know you'll have to in the long run, so it might as well be now."

It might have worked, for Brazos with his empty hands, powerful frame and easy-going, man-to-man approach was something more akin to the simple, rough-hewn Irish laborers than the handsome Benedict with his fancy waistcoat and gun. But just as it seemed they might give way, Old Billy Murphy pushed through them with a drunken curse and poked at Brazos with his crutch.

Acting instinctively, Brazos pushed the crutch aside. Murphy staggered, hit his stump as he fell and shrieked. There was a rumble of anger and then buck-toothed Cliff Moran lunged forward and took a smack at Brazos' jaw.

Brazos' right fist blurred and Moran went down like a poled steer. Another man rushed in, presented his face to a jolting left and reeled back with flailing arms, dripping crimson from a mashed nose. As a third attacker buckled at the knees to an almost casual right cross to the jaw, Brazos was beginning to enjoy it.

Then Paddy Clancy joined the lists. Clancy had been determined to stand back and give orders as befitted a leader, but the sound of thumping fists was a siren song he couldn't resist; so, leaping over Billy Murphy who was still cursing and groaning on the ground, he bore down on Brazos like a runaway locomotive.

Turning to meet the charge, Brazos knew immediately that massive, iron-ribbed Clancy was a worthy adversary. So did Benedict, who jerked on the reins to bring his horse in close, and then as Clancy rushed by, clipped him hard across the skull with his gun barrel.

It was a blow that would have knocked a normal man bowlegged. All it did to Clancy was throw him off stride. But that was enough for Brazos. Before Clancy could get his balance the big Texan lunged forward and sledged a pounding right to the jaw that sent

51

Clancy staggering back into Benedict's horse where Benedict cold-cocked him with the six-gun, knocking him to his knees.

Spinning the gun on his finger, Benedict triggered at the sky. "All right, that will do it," he said with authority as the crash of the shot rolled away.

After a hanging moment of uncertainty, the blue-denimed ranks opened up. Benedict motioned Kingston through to the gates, then backed his horse and picked up Brazos' appaloosa. Brazos made an offer to help Clancy off his knees, but the stunned giant knocked his outstretched hand violently aside. Brazos shrugged, took his reins from Benedict in silence and went on with Bullpup as Kingston swung the gates open.

Only then did Benedict house his gun. He leaned forward in his saddle, his crossed arms on the saddle-horn. "No hard feelings, gentlemen. Now, why don't you all stroll down to the saloon and have a nice cold beer? You can tell the barkeep I'll be good for the first round."

The miners had been off balance from the moment Clancy had gone down, but the sudden transformation in Benedict from cold-eyed menace to amiable friendliness took what little steam they might have had left right out of them.

Confused and crestfallen, they helped their companions to their feet and in a sullen, silent blue mass, began to slowly move off.

"Magnificent," Kingston exulted as Benedict joined him in the gateway. "You handled them brilliantly, Duke. And you, too, Hank." He laughed. "Did you see the look on Clancy's face when he went down? He couldn't believe it."

Benedict glanced at Brazos, then both stared after the miners. Walking unaided now, Clancy was glaring back over his shoulder at them and even at that distance they could feel the impact of the giant's hatred. Both felt it might be a little early in the day to start laughing at big Paddy Clancy.

FOUR

CLANCY

Half an hour after the break-in, six of Kingston's Regulators under Art Shadie arrived at the Motherlode packing enough artillery to equip a small revolution. They took up vantage points around the mine in case the miners decided to try to re-take the place. As Benedict and Foley Kingston inspected the offices and installations for signs of damage, Brazos sat on his spurs in the shade of the porch overhang of the main office building. A cigarette dangling from his lips, Brazos playfully tossed pebbles at a drowsing Bullpup.

"Everything seems in order," Brazos heard Kingston say to Benedict as the two emerged from the steep-roofed wagon house and walked towards a towering ore crusher. "Lucky for them, too."

He didn't catch Benedict's response, mainly because he wasn't much interested, and secondly because he had just sighted a man approaching down the road towards the gates. A man dressed in a miner's blue denim.

Uncoiling lazily to his feet, Brazos stretched powerful arms and looked across at Shadie and his men. They were too busy gabbing about the victory to notice the solitary walker, and Kingston and Benedict were out of sight beyond the crushing machine. Brazos stepped out into the brutal sun and, with Bullpup trailing, slouched across to the gates to see what the fellow wanted.

Brazos recognized the miner as one of Clancy's men, a quiet-looking joker of about fifty who Brazos recalled trying to pacify the others when the trouble broke out.

"Forget somethin', friend?" Brazos said with a half grin as the man trudged up.

The miner answered the Texan's smile a little wearily and moved into the shade beside him to mop at his face with a dark blue bandanna.

"Not really, young feller," he said in a pleasantly soft voice.. "You're Brazos, aren't you? Delaney's my name, Shamus Delaney."

Before Brazos could answer, Shadie's men spotted the miner and started to raise hell. Turning from the hips, Brazos shouted back to them to shut up, then he grinned at Delaney again.

"Boys are a little jumpy, Shamus. Somethin' we can do for you?"

"I came back to see if I mightn't have a little talk with Mr. Kingston. Here he comes now."

Foley Kingston certainly was coming. Outstripping Benedict, the big man was striding towards them, his face red and angry in the shade of his broad-brimmed white hat.

"Delaney!" he barked. "What do you think you're doing here?"

"He's come to parley," Brazos said.

"Indeed I have, Mr. Kingston," Delaney said. "I'm not sure if it's the time or place but—"

"You're damned right it's not," Kingston snorted. "We just got rid of you law-breaking troublemakers and we don't want you showing your faces around here again."

"Perhaps we could hear what Mr. Delaney has to say, Foley," Benedict suggested.

The Irishman shot a grateful look at Benedict and said, "Mr. Kingston, I just wanted to be sayin' that after what happened here today, maybe it's time we tried sittin' down and talkin' things over again. I think you know that I've never really supported Clancy and his friends, and I'm thinkin' we might all be lucky that nobody got killed here today. Don't you think now might be a good time to talk before the whole thing gets out of hand?"

The proposal sounded reasonable to Brazos and Benedict—but not to Foley Kingston.

"I've no intention of talking with you, Delaney," he said coldly. "The time for talking is past and now you and your rebellious friends can just sit back and reap what you have sown."

"But, Mr. Kingston—"

"That's all, Delaney. Now move on or I'll have you moved."

Delaney looked at Benedict and Brazos, seemed about to say something more, then turned and trudged off down the glaring stretch of road.

"I don't understand it, Foley," Duke Benedict said after a long silence. "He seemed as if he genuinely wanted to talk."

"They're as crafty as coyotes, those Irish, Duke," Kingston said. "Not one of them is to be trusted, believe me." His smile returned. "But let's not worry about Delaney and his ilk at the moment. This is a special day of achievement and we're all going to enjoy it. I'm going to the office in town, but before I do I want your assurance that you'll come up to the house this evening." Kingston's winning smile flashed at Brazos. "I'm going to put on a victory supper, Hank, and I've told Duke I insist on you two attending."

Brazos looked at Benedict who said quietly, "We'll be there, Foley."

"Good, good," Kingston replied. Then as he turned to go, "And tonight you'll definitely meet my wife, boys. I'm certain you'll find that quite a treat. I know Rhea is going to be as happy about our victory as I am."

Standing on either side of the gateway, neither man spoke until Kingston had ridden out with Regulators Hasty and Miller and was dusting towards town. Then Brazos said:

"I don't figure it, Yank. Kingston acts like he don't give a damn whether them miners come back to work or not. How the hell's he expect to get this outfit goin' again if he won't even talk to 'em?"

There was no reply from Benedict. He was thinking hard about Foley Kingston. He was aware, far more sharply than at any time before, that Foley hadn't completely leveled with him about the set-up in Spargo. Foley was holding a few cards back in this game which, as dealer, he likely had a right to do. But Benedict hoped one of the cards wasn't a joker.

"There, pet, does that feel better?"

"Much better, Mother," Clancy said. "Now I'll—"

"Now don't start fidgetin', you big lump. I haven't put the bandage around your head yet."

"It's all right, Mother."

"Sure and who knows what's best for ye, son, you or your mother?"

"You do, Mother, but—"

"Then shut your great gapin' gob and let me be for gettin' on with it," Mother Clancy snapped in a characteristically swift switch from solicitude to bossiness.

"Do ye think a body's got nothin' better to be doin' than patchin' up your bumps and bruises all day long?"

With a sigh of resignation, Clancy fell silent and let the skinny woman get on with the job of strapping up his big hard head where Duke Benedict's six-gun barrel had made violent contact an hour back. There was a two-inch split in the hairline that had bled a little, but he'd had fifty times worse and laughed about it, though there was no telling his mother that. She treated him like an overgrown child all the time, and doubly so at times like this.

Soon Mother Clancy's brisk wrinkled little hands finished their task and she stood back from the stool her son sat on in the middle of the tiny kitchen to admire her handiwork. Seated, Clancy was a fraction taller than his mother standing. She was barely over five feet tall, a skinny, wrinkled, fiercely energetic little Irishwoman in a black grannie dress and high-button boots. A clay pipe jutted from her jaw. Her face was like intricately wrinkled parchment with two black nails driven into it for eyes, and her gray hair was pulled severely back in a bun. Though she wouldn't weigh a hundred pounds pulled from a lake, Mother Clancy had the authority of a field gun and there were few men in town who hadn't trembled under the caustic lick of her Killarney tongue at one time or another—and that went double for Clancy.

"All right," she said, "now tell me how you got it cracked."

Clancy rose and had to bend his bandaged head to protect it from a ceiling that had been built to accommodate men of normal size.

"I told ye, Mother, I fell over in the street."

"Ye great lyin' spalpeen! You're thinkin' a body's so old and squinty she can't be tellin' a pistol-whippin' when she sees one? Who hit ye—and why?"

"I fell over and that's the truth."

"I should wash your mouth out," the woman snapped, but her old face sagged with worry as she turned to her stove. She had heard rumors—a word here, a snippet there, but that was all. What did she understand about strikes and suchlike? But she was aware that her son was deeply involved in a dangerous situation and she prayed every night on the beads that he would not come to real harm.

She was fixing coffee for him when a knock sounded on the door. Clancy opened the door to O'Rourke who had a message from uptown: Ace Beauford wanted to see Clancy.

"All right," Clancy said quickly, "I'll be comin'. Wait out at the gate. You know how mother is about ye."

"What's that gaspin', hackin' little Orangeman want with ye?" Mother Clancy snapped as the door closed.

"Well, he just come to remind me the lads are havin' a meetin' at the hotel to—"

"Liar! I heard him say somethin' about Beauford. What does that black-eyed divil always be wantin' with ye these days? Ye know I've got no time for him."

Clancy threw up his hands in exasperation. "Blast it all, half the time you're sayin' you're deaf as a post, but you hear more'n a jackrabbit I'm thinkin'."

"I hear enough and see enough to know that you're lettin' yourself be dragged down to somethin' way over your head in this misbegotten town of trouble."

For once Mother Clancy was off the mark. It was her darling son who was in the forefront of the trouble in Spargo—dragging down a lot of other men who were as much in awe of his crushing fists as he was of his mother's waspish tongue.

"You fret too much," he told her, rolling the sleeves of his plaid shirt up above his mighty biceps as he went out. "I know what I'm doin'."

"That's what your drunken sot of a father used to say," she called after him from the doorway. "Until the night they brought him home on a door. Now ye don't be gettin' into any more bother and don't be sneakin' in late, hear?"

Clancy scowled murderously as he strode through the gate and tramped down poverty-stricken Bonanza Street with O'Rourke trotting at his heels. He was so used to his mother's tirades that he didn't notice them half the time, but he hated her calling him down within earshot of anybody.

They'd gone fifty yards before he noticed O'Rourke was grinning.

"What are ye smilin' at, ye fool?" he growled.

"Don't be gettin' home late," O'Rourke mimicked. "And don't be gettin' into trouble."

O'Rourke should have known better. Hardly breaking stride, Clancy clapped him to the side of the head, knocking him sideways. Eyes rolling, O'Rourke crashed into Buck Jackson's fragile front fence which collapsed about him with a great clatter as he went down.

Alerted by the crash, people came running out to see what was going on. Clancy paid them no heed. Arms swinging, big boots covering five feet at a stride, he went on until he reached the Delaney house, where Shamus Delaney and his dark-haired daughter stood on their front porch staring at him.

Clancy stopped at the fence. His ferocious intimidating stare, which just about everybody but his mother was familiar with in Spargo, stabbed accusingly at Delaney.

"So, Delaney, they're tellin' me you went back to the mine today on your own after I said you weren't to. Is it the truth?"

Delaney came down his path, but his slender, pretty daughter remained on the verandah.

"Sure, I went back, Clancy," he said in his soft brogue. "I thought I might be able to talk with Foley Kingston."

"But he wouldn't listen, would he?"

"No … no, he wouldn't."

"Then next time you might follow my orders." Clancy poked Delaney in the chest with an iron finger and prodded him back a step. "In fact, next time, if you don't, I might take it personal and feel I got to crack a few of your old chicken bones. Understand me, Delaney?"

Pale-faced, Delaney said, "I was only tryin' to—"

"Don't try anything," Clancy warned, and with a cold stare at the girl, strode off.

Tricia Delaney hurried down to her father and took his arm. "Oh, Dad, did he hurt you?"

"Of course not, me darlin'." He patted her hand. "Clancy's just a little worked up over what happened at the mine is all. He means no harm."

"He does and you know it, Dad," the girl said. "I could just see by his face how angry he is about what's happened. What do you think he'll do about those men, Brazos and Benedict?"

Delaney sighed. "It's hard to say what he'll do, Tricia."

"But we know he'll be doing something."

Delaney suddenly felt the full weight of his years. "Aye, he'll be doing something, child. Never was one to take somethin' lyin' down was Clancy …"

"A toast," said a beaming Foley Kingston from the head of the great dining table. He twirled the wine glass in his fingers and grinned boyishly. "Forgive the immodesty, but I'm proposing this toast to me—yes, to me—for having the good sense to ask my friend Duke for assistance, without which today's success could certainly not have been achieved."

Benedict and Brazos lifted their glasses, but Rhea Kingston left her glass on the table. Rhea, breath-takingly beautiful in a figure-hugging white evening dress with diamonds glittering at wrists and throat, stared across the table at Benedict.

Rhea Kingston was intrigued. She had agreed to dine with her husband and his two guests tonight only because Foley had insisted. He had painted a glow-ing picture of Duke Benedict, but she'd still expected him to be a cold-eyed killer with the stamp of his trade all over him. Instead she found herself confronted by a gentleman of style, wit and charm who was probably the most handsome man she had ever met.

"I do believe it is my turn now, Foley," Benedict said, getting to his feet. Gray eyes smiling, he lifted his glass to Rhea. "A toast, gentlemen, to the rarest of all God's creatures, a truly beautiful woman."

Rhea was angry with herself for blushing. Foley beamed proudly, but Cole Kingston frowned. As for Brazos, he was thinking it would be a lot more com-fortable down town at the Lucky Cuss or the Silver King with his fist around a beer instead of listening to all this hoopla and watching Benedict and Kingston's luscious wife devour each other with their eyes.

"Beautifully put, Duke, beautifully put," Kingston said as they resumed their seats. "And now, before I bring the musicians in to entertain us, I have some serious announcements to make."

"Don't you think you've talked enough for one night, Foley?" Rhea said in her husky voice.

"Patience, my dear," Kingston said. "I'm sure this will interest you, too." Kingston made a tent with his fingers and looked at Brazos and Benedict. "Gentlemen, I could tell today that you were puzzled when I showed no interest in talking with Shamus Delaney after we got the better of them at the Motherlode. Right?"

They nodded together, and Rhea Kingston looked curious.

"Very well," Foley continued, "I think the time has come to explain, and I'm sure that what I have to tell you will clarify a great number of things in your minds. The fact of the matter is, I have no interest in negotiating with Delaney, Clancy or anybody else, for I don't intend that the miners will return to work in my mine except on my terms. I have other plans."

"Strike-breakers?"

It was Cole Kingston who spoke. They glanced sharply at him, then back to Kingston who was smiling.

"Exactly, Cole. Strike-breakers." Kingston turned to his wife. "You recall the other evening when Shadie returned from the south and you were curious, my dear? Well, he had been to Granite to see a labor dealer named Heck Lafe. Lafe told Shadie he could let me have a hundred Mexican laborers to work the Motherlode—at only one dollar a day per man. I wired Lafe to stand by with the Mexicans. Now, thanks to Duke, and Hank, too, of course, I can send for them. What do you think of that?"

Rhea Kingston looked as if she didn't know quite what to think of it, but Benedict found words quickly.

"Won't bringing in cheap labor antagonize the strikers, Foley? Isn't there another way?"

"No, Duke," said Kingston, looking every inch the man with the big stick now as he slapped the table top. "I've been convinced from the start that the strikers are out to ruin me and it's not going to happen. I'm not going to be bullied or blackmailed by a bunch of illiterate shanty Irish. They've had their fun and now it's my turn."

Benedict glanced at Brazos who looked as if he were having trouble following Kingston's words. Cole Kingston seemed apprehensive. Rhea was now staring at Foley with an intent expression that was unreadable. Benedict was frowning as he turned his gaze back to Kingston.

"Foley, what you do here is your business, I suppose, but something just struck me. There has to be big trouble here in Spargo if you try to bring cheap labor in. Is that why you really sent for me? To have me on hand when that particular trouble breaks?"

"Exactly, Duke, and I make no apologies. Of course, if you don't agree with what I'm doing, you're free to pull out. You're under no obligation to ride for me. I trust you understand that?"

Benedict had to smile at the subtle use of the word *obligation*. He was obliged right enough, and Kingston was reminding him of it. Because Foley had dragged him unconscious from the path of a Rebel cavalry charge at Bull Run, he was expected to stand at Foley's shoulder here in Spargo. Obligation was the word.

"I understand, Foley," he murmured, the soft candlelight gleaming on his black hair as he bent his head and took out his cigar case. "I'm still with you."

"Fine," Kingston beamed, "fine." He glanced around the table. "Well, my news seems to have had a sobering effect, though I'm not sure why. Cole, go tell the boys to bring their instruments in, will you? What we need here is some music and some more wine. Come on, everybody, cheer up—this is a celebration, not a wake."

FIVE

POVERTY STREET

"There's not a man among ye!" Old Billy Murphy told the drinkers lining the bar of the Lucky Cuss Saloon. He tried to make a contemptuous gesture and almost fell, for he was very drunk. "Ye let a pair of gunnies walk right over the top of ye, then ye go runnin' off with your tails betwixt your legs."

None of the men at the bar had been at the gates of the Motherlode earlier that day, but that didn't worry Billy.

"It's enough to make a decent man want to be sick," Billy went on. "Two men—two men made ye run—a big oaf of a clown and a fancy-mouthed dandy in a whorehouse vest."

"You'd show 'im if you was of a mind, wouldn't you, Billy?" a hatchet-faced cowboy called out derisively.

"You'd cut Benedict right down to size if you just had the time, wouldn't you?"

"I would only for this," Billy said, raising his crutch. "I'd shame all of ye …"

His voice trailed off and his stare went blank, whisky and pain and rage overcoming him so that he couldn't recall what he'd been so angry about, even when he bent to his drink and the butt of Tommy's rusty old Colt stuck into his ribs.

"Fancy-mouthed dandy," he muttered, and wished he could remember who he meant.

Brazos turned at Bullpup's growl to see Cole Kingston coming along the lamp lit gallery.

"Make a fine couple dancing, don't they, Hank?" the young man said with a nod at the window.

Brazos looked through the window and saw Rhea and Benedict moving gracefully across the floor to the strains of a Spanish love song. It was some time after nine, and it seemed to Brazos they'd been dancing for a hell of a long time. He'd quickly become bored and had quit the room to get some air. But Foley Kingston didn't look bored. He was clapping time to the music, smiling at the dancers and taking down one drink after another.

"I've seen worse I guess," Brazos grunted. He twirled his hat by the throat strap for a minute then turned his back on the brightly lit room. "This ain't really my speed, kid. I'm headin' back to the hotel. Say goodnight to the folks for me, will you?"

"Sure." The young man smiled engagingly as Brazos moved to go. "Say, I wonder if you'd mind doing something for me, Hank?"

"What's that?"

"You haven't met Miss Tricia Delaney yet, have you?"

"Reckon not. She kin to Shamus Delaney, the pilgrim we was talkin' to at the mine today?"

"His daughter. They live on Bonanza Street, next to an old bakery. I don't like asking you to do this, Hank, but I was supposed to see Miss Delaney tonight, only Dad decided to have this evening for you and Duke, and I haven't been able to get a message to her that I can't come. I'd go myself but Dad might notice me missing."

"Say no more, Cole, it's good as done."

"Thanks, Hank." Kingston glanced back at the house. "And don't mention this to anybody, eh? You see, Tricia and I were planning to get married. Then all the trouble started with the miners and Dad ordered me not to see her again because she's Shamus' daughter. You understand?"

"Sure."

"Good … Come on, I'll walk to the gate with you." The sounds of the music faded behind them as they strolled towards the wrought-iron gates that were emblazoned with a scrolled K. The night's full moon etched the yard's pines and cottonwoods darkly against the sky.

Brazos had a hunch that Cole Kingston hadn't said all he had to say. Then, when the young man halted at the gates, Brazos learned he'd guessed right.

"How long do you and Duke plan to stay on?" Cole asked.

Brazos shrugged. "As long as it takes, I reckon. Why?

"Well, I—I guess I wouldn't say this if I didn't feel you were both good men, but … well, I wish you'd pull out. Now."

"Why?"

Cole gestured at the house with one hand and the town with the other. "Because this whole thing's a dirty mess, Hank. There's no wrongs and rights here in Spargo. There's faults on both sides and things are going to get worse than ever when news of the strike-breakers gets around."

Brazos hazed a grin. "You're not sayin' your pappy's at fault here, are you, Cole?"

"I'm not saying anything more than what I've said—that you and Benedict should ride out, Hank, before it's too late."

"Sorry, kid. Benedict's here to do a job of work for your pappy and I'm helpin' him do it. But thanks, anyway."

Cole Kingston sighed as he watched the heavy-shouldered Texan walk down the moonlit trail with his ugly dog trotting before him. Cole looked at the moon and thought of nights when he and Tricia Delaney had strolled arm-in-arm down Johnny Street. But that was before the air of Spargo became infected with the poison stink of hate and violence.

"I'm not made of glass, Duke."

"Pardon?"

Rhea Kingston's slanted green eyes glittered challengingly. "I mean you can hold me a little closer without fear of my breaking."

Benedict glanced at Kingston as he whirled Rhea past the corner where the three Mexican musicians played.

Rhea laughed. "Foley doesn't care. He's not the jealous kind. Besides, you're his friend." She moved closer and he felt the pressure of her magnificent body against him. "See? It doesn't hurt, does it?"

That wasn't exactly true, Benedict mused as he glanced down at the deep, mysterious cleft between her breasts, but he felt it would be less painful all around if they maintained a discreet distance between them.

Rhea pouted prettily when he moved her away from him. From then on, Benedict tried hard to keep his eyes from straying further south than Rhea Kingston's lovely chin.

Bonanza Street was a narrow lane with houses lined on each side like rabbit hutches. Down here it was hessian at the windows, potholes in the street and patches in the pants. The odor that hung over Bonanza Street was the smell of poverty, a scent Hank Brazos recalled from his threadbare Texas childhood.

He found the Delaney house without any trouble. As he went up the short path to the front door, he noted the neatness of the yard and the porch.

Darkly attractive Tricia Delaney answered the door. She startled Hank by inviting him in for a cup of coffee after he delivered Cole Kingston's message.

Turning his battered hat in his hands, Brazos grinned ruefully in the weak yellow oil light drifting from the hall. "I reckon you didn't get my name, Missy. I'm Hank Brazos and I'm workin' for—"

"I know who you are, Mr. Brazos," she said in a voice that had just a touch of Irish in it. "You and Mr. Benedict were pointed out to me on the street this morning. You're still welcome."

She stepped aside and gestured down the hall, but Brazos stood there uncertainly. Then a voice called, "Who is it, honey?" and Shamus Delaney appeared with a pipe in his mouth.

"This is Mr. Brazos, Father," the girl said with a smile. "I believe you two have already met. Mr. Brazos has just brought a message down from Cole that he can't see me tonight, but he doesn't seem to want to come in for a cup of coffee in return for his kindness."

"What's the matter, son?" Delaney said. "Don't you like coffee?"

Brazos shuffled his feet. "Why, I guess I like coffee better'n just about anythin', but—"

"Son," the Irishman cut him off, "I'm not for holdin' any grudge about what happened at the Motherlode today if you're not. The truth is, I was never in favor of us takin' over the mine in the first place and I'm damned glad Mr. Kingston took it back. Now will you share our hospitality?"

"I surely will," Brazos grinned. "Bullpup, set and wait."

"Oh, no," Tricia Delaney said, then she reached down and patted Bullpup's head. She further surprised Brazos by smiling when Bullpup licked at her hand with a fat pink tongue that had the texture of sandpaper. "He's such a beautiful, manly dog. Let him come in and I'll give him something to eat."

If there was one certain way of getting on the friendly side of Hank Brazos it was by making a fuss over his dog, an animal so ugly he'd been known to cause full-scale panic amongst womenfolk just by making an appearance. "I thank you kindly, Missy." Brazos smiled and entered the parlor.

He was still there an hour later with four cups of good black coffee and about a dozen fat sourdough biscuits in him. Shamus and Tricia Delaney, drawn out by Brazos' questions, proved to be mines of information as well as gracious hosts.

Brazos learned that Paddy Clancy bossed the miners, not because he was popular, but because he could lick any three good men with his fists and was ready to prove it at the drop of a challenge. At first, Delaney was unofficial leader of the miners, but then Clancy took over, started the strike and kept it going. Delaney made it clear that, though most of the strikers disliked and feared Clancy, they supported the idea of the strike because the Motherlode, due to years of improper maintenance, was a deathtrap for miners.

When Brazos asked how the men could strike for so long and still eat, Delaney said there was an "angel" in Spargo who helped pay the miners' food bills at the store. Delaney didn't know the identity of this philanthropist nor the reason for his generosity, but he had a strong suspicion that it was Ace Beauford, owner of the Silver King Saloon and close friend of Clancy.

Mental agility not being his long suit, Brazos found the situation perplexing. But Delaney had more for him to think about. The Irishman, supported by his daughter who sat off to one side feeding Bullpup leftovers, insisted that none of the rank-and-file miners had any knowledge of the ambush attempt by Billy Murphy's son, though Delaney conceded that Paddy Clancy's hand could be in it somewhere.

It was then that Brazos steered the conversation around to the standoff between the strikers and Foley Kingston. Brazos understood Kingston's angle, following disclosure of his plan to bring in cheap labor, but he couldn't figure out why Clancy seemed so dead set against finding a solution.

Delaney could throw no light on that, but, knowing Clancy, he said that gain had to be in it somewhere. "He might be big and foul-mouthed and hot-tempered, Hank," he warned, adding a little whisky to his coffee, "but Paddy Clancy is no fool. There's them who've thought he was and they've paid a heavy price for it."

Waving aside Tricia's offer of a fifth coffee, Brazos rolled a cigarette and sat smoking in silence for some time, going over what Delaney had told him. Uppermost in his thoughts was the certainty of bloodshed in Spargo when Kingston brought in his strike-breakers from the south, and the fact that he and Benedict were going to be in the thick of it. Were the miners in the right? Had Kingston driven them to strike? Was Kingston wearing the black hat? And, most important, was the mine too dangerous to work or wasn't it?

He eventually put this question to Delaney who shrugged. "I suppose there's only one way you could be knowin' that for sure, Hank, and that's to see for yourself."

Brazos pursed his lips thoughtfully for a moment. "Mebbe you're right at that, Shamus. And mebbe that's just what I'll do."

Delaney studied his face, then shrugged. "Well, there's nothin' stoppin' you takin' a look, I suppose, though I doubt if Foley Kingston would want you sniffin about down there."

"Mebbe I won't bother tellin' him until I've had me a look-see." Brazos glanced at the clock on the wall. It was eleven-thirty. "Mebbe I'll mosey on down to the Motherlode now while I'm in the mood. Want to come along, Shamus?"

"Me?"

"Sure, why not? I could get Shadie or somebody there to take me down, but if things are as bad as you say, mebbe they'd make sure I didn't see the bad parts."

Delaney looked at his daughter and she nodded her dark head. "Well, all right, why not? Sure, we'll go along to the Motherlode together and you'll see for yourself that things are just like I say."

Foley Kingston's voice, thick with whisky and anger, drifted down the corridor and seeped under the door of the room where Duke Benedict was taking off his coat and loosening his four-in-hand tie.

"Rhea, damn you, open your door!"

If Rhea Kingston replied, Benedict didn't hear it. He hung up his coat and was unbuckling his heavy double gun rig when Kingston's voice sounded again:

"All right, you cold bitch, sleep by yourself then! Who cares!"

Benedict heard a door bang with an impact that rocked the house. He grinned without humor as he hung his gun rig on the bed post and unbuttoned his waistcoat. That was the risk you ran staying overnight with people: you were likely to hear and see more than you wanted to. He would have returned to the Spargo Hotel, but Foley had insisted that he stay, and Kingston had been too drunk to take a refusal without an argument.

Benedict felt weary but not sleepy. In his shirtsleeves, he stretched out on the bed in the guest room and locked his hands behind his head. The evening had been pleasant enough, though Foley had drunk too much and Rhea had been a little indiscreet in flirting with him. She was certainly a looker. She had the loveliest pair of … eyes … he'd seen in too many months.

He wondered where Brazos had got to. Cole had told him that Brazos had left around nine. Bored, no doubt. He'd probably gone off to a saloon to get a bellyful of beer and talk about the price of beef with cowboys. That would be more his speed.

He got up to light a last cigar from the lamp, then turned it out. Angling bars of moonlight came through the French doors giving onto the upstairs balcony. Pacing the floor and smoking, he had the feeling sleep was going to prove elusive. Too many things to think about. Like what was going to happen when Foley brought in his strike-breakers.

Time passed. His cigar was smoked out and he was stretched out on the bed again, staring at the ceiling, more wide awake than before. Out in the mountains, wolves were howling.

Finally Benedict swung his boots to the floor and went onto the balcony, the night wind rippling his shirtsleeves. All around him the great house was quiet, and few lights burned down in Spargo.

He drew back from the balustrade at a sound from below. Peering through the columns, he saw a cloaked figure hurry across the lawn. A cowl hood prevented him from seeing the night walker's face, but when a gust of wind pressed the cloak's dark folds against a richly curved figure, he had no trouble at all in recognizing Rhea Kingston.

He straightened slowly as the woman disappeared in the direction of town. Was it any business of his if Rhea Kingston was sneaking to town at one in the morning?

That raised a second question. Wasn't anything and everything connected with Foley Kingston his business now that Kingston had hired his guns?

Quickly he put on his coat, hat and gunbelt.

SIX

ACE IN THE PACK

"Oh, darling, you know what that does to me."

His lips moved over her naked breasts. A low flame in a ruby glass filled the room with a misty crimson glow. It gleamed on the dark furniture, the heavy drapes that weren't quite closed, the clock that showed two-fifteen, and the man and the woman on the bed.

The man, stripped to the waist, had a lean body that put the lie to his silver hair. His face, both handsome and cruel, was softened now with desire.

The woman was naked. Her arms were out flung beneath rich auburn hair that spread out like a dark fan around her head. Her eyes were closed as his lips caressed her large, pink-budded breasts. The dim light gleamed softly on the satiny skin of long legs and clung to dramatically rounded curves. Beautiful at any time, she was doubly so in that ruby light, both to her lover and to the man with his eye at the thin chink in the curtains.

Suddenly the man stiffened, his head jerked up to stare at the drapes.

"Ace," the woman murmured, her voice dreamy and husky, "what is it?"

"I thought I heard something," he whispered, sliding his feet to the floor.

She sat up as he took a small Derringer from the night table. "I didn't hear anything, Ace."

"Maybe it was just my imagination," he said softly, padding for the door. "But I'll take a look just in case."

He jerked the door open and stepped onto the long wooden balcony that encircled the upstairs quarters at the back of the Silver King Saloon. The balcony was empty. Gun at the ready, he went to the railing and leaned over to peer into the black pits of moon shadow below.

"Anybody there?" he called.

No answer. He turned and frowned when he saw the chink in the drapes. A door opened two rooms down and Ace Beauford's gunman bodyguard appeared, tousle-headed and with a Colt .45 in his fist.

"That you singin' out, Ace? What's wrong?"

"Just thought I heard somebody sneaking about," Beauford replied. "But I guess I was wrong. Go back to bed, Holly."

The gunfighter twirled his six-gun on his finger, grinned and disappeared inside. Then the woman called to Beauford.

"Coming, Rhea," he replied, took a final glance about, then went in and closed the door behind him.

Once more silence enveloped the Silver King. Two minutes passed, then a dark shape emerged from beneath the balcony and stood for a moment looking up at the window where a dim red light softly burned.

Benedict turned and made his way silently along the alley flanking the saloon. Reaching Johnny Street, he paused to light his third cigar of that early Thursday before strolling off slowly, and more than a little thoughtfully, for Kingston Hill.

Duke Benedict strolled through the slanting sunlight towards the Spargo House Hotel. He was decked out in his black broadcloth suit, hand-tooled dress boots and twenty-dollar hat. He doffed his hat to a passing matron who clucked and flushed and hurried on her way like a startled hen. Benedict looked rested and relaxed and in the pink of condition, despite the fact that he'd had less than four hours' sleep.

It was mid-morning and Johnny Street was busy with horsemen and wagons and men afoot. Groups of strikers from the Motherlode stood in the verandah shade along the far side of the street. There was a racket of catcalls and whistles as two sporting girls from Coyote Street promenaded past the freight depot and stopped to look in a store window. Somebody had told Benedict that business had fallen off alarmingly in Coyote Street since the Motherlode closed down. He supposed the girls would be as happy as anybody else when things got back to normal.

Mrs. Daphne Hogg, the portly wife of mine host at the Spargo House, looked up from her ledger and beamed when she saw who had entered the hotel.

"Good morning, Mr. Benedict." She wagged a plump finger and added roguishly, "My, but you're a bold one and no mistake, aren't you?"

Resting his hands on the desk, Benedict cocked an eyebrow. "Pardon?"

She pointed to the clock. "Ten o'clock in the morning and you just getting in. My, my."

"Well, I'm sorry to disappoint you, dear lady, but I spent the night with friends."

She giggled girlishly. "That's what you tell me. Oh, Mr. Benedict, you must think I came down in the last shower. A fine looking man like you, staying with friends? Now, now …"

"Of course you are right, my astute Mrs. Hogg," he said with a wicked grin. "As they say: The way of the eagle is in the air, the way of the ship is on the sea, and the way of a man is with a maid."

"Oh, Mr. Benedict, you *are* bold."

"Indubitably," murmured Benedict. And then, feeling he'd just about exhausted giddy Mrs. Hogg's possibilities, asked, "Is Mr. Brazos abroad yet?"

"Oh, yes, he is, out at the bath-house. He's another naughty one, too."

Moving for the rear door, Benedict paused. "Oh, and why is that?"

"He didn't get in until three himself."

"Is that a fact? Well, that is curious."

The bath-house, a circular, red-painted wooden edifice with a tin roof, stood in the center of the hotel's back yard. As Benedict stepped onto the plank walk that led to the door, he heard sounds of violence coming from the little building, and then someone shouted:

"Come back, you flea-infested, pot-lickin', camp-robbin' Judas Iscariot son-of-a-bitch or I'll god-damn split your crutch to Christmas!"

This was followed by a growl, a great splash and more lurid cursing from Brazos.

Unable to contain his curiosity any longer, Benedict opened the bath-house door and gaped. The walls of the twelve-foot wide bath-house were splattered with soap and the floor was covered with water. In the center of the room, Brazos, drenched to the skin and wearing a mask of froth, was kneeling by the stout wooden tub wrestling with a furiously struggling, fully lathered Bullpup who was in the tub, growling, wriggling and spluttering.

There was just time for this to register with Benedict before the timbers shook with the blast of Brazos' bellow.

"Shut that motherless door, damn blast your eyes!"

He tried, but too late. Bullpup had been given a heady glimpse of sunshine and wide open spaces. Bursting out of Brazos' wildly clutching arms like a greased pig, Bullpup raced full tilt for the door roaring like a mad bull, and drove headlong into the closing gap in the door with desperate impact.

The door was thumped open and the edge caught Benedict's ear. Cursing, he drove his shoulder into the door, but the powerful hound was already halfway out. Bullpup's head swung and iron molars clashed a hair's breadth from Benedict's pants leg. Benedict leapt back instinctively, and the dog surged through.

"Cretin of a beast!" Benedict snarled and aimed a vicious kick that missed by a full yard as Bullpup, with the heady air of freedom in his lungs, streaked across the yard for the gate in a white blur of soapsuds. All Benedict's wild kick caught was Hank Brazos' shin as he came barreling through the bathhouse doorway in Bullpup's wake, cursing like a muleskinner. Arms flailing wildly, Brazos staggered ten yards across the yard, desperately fighting for balance before he tripped on a plank, crashed down, turned a complete somersault and came to rest on his broad wet back with his big boots sticking out through the gateway.

Silence.

Benedict tenderly touched his ear, then smiled at the half-dozen gaping faces that had come to stare from the back stoop.

"Bathing the dog," he explained. "Got away."

Still not looking too sure that all the commotion and cursing could possibly have come from simply giving a dog a bath, they watched as Brazos hauled himself to his feet, plastered with dirt. Then, shaking their heads, they went back inside.

"Nice timin', Benedict," Brazos growled sarcastically as he came across the yard.

"How the devil was I to know you were bathing the monster? As far as I recall, he hasn't been washed in six months."

"On account of it takes me six months to work up the energy," Brazos shot back. "Well, he's good and gone now," he added resignedly. "You eaten yet?"

"Not really," Benedict said, sober now as he took out a fresh Havana. "I was offered breakfast at Kingston's, but I didn't have the appetite."

Steam rising off him as he stood in the sun, Brazos looked at his trail partner closely. "You, too, eh? Funny, I was off my chow this mornin'."

"Impossible. Never been heard of."

Brazos let that pass. He was dead serious now. "Yank, I got a few things to tell you about last night."

"That's a coincidence," Benedict said, "for I have a thing or two to tell you about last night, too. Why don't you get a fresh shirt on and meet me over at Mulligan's eatery and we can compare notes?"

"You got a deal."

Benedict knew the situation was serious when Brazos ordered only a cup of hot and black coffee despite the aromatic temptations of Mulligan's eatery.

Behind his long counter, Mulligan himself, decked out in a greasy apron and a cocked chef's hat, was busily occupied knocking up a batch of son-of-a-gun stew—the sort of fare that mostly could lure a hearty cowboy trencherman like Brazos from the next county.

Even Benedict, who considered son-of-a-gun stew not up to the standard demanded of his educated palate, found his mouth watering a little as the rich scent filled the air. But Brazos didn't seem to notice, so Benedict found himself wondering what sort of calamity had occurred to put his partner off his food.

"I took a look over the Motherlode last night," Brazos said suddenly. "With Shamus Delaney."

"Not exactly my idea of an entertaining night. But so?"

"So it stinks."

"You'll have to elucidate."

"Eh?"

"Explain … exactly how does it stink?"

"It's a death trap, Yank. I don't know a power about mines, but anybody could see that it needs re-timberin' from backside to breakfast. I tell you I was damned glad to get back up out of there in one piece—and we was just lookin' around."

Benedict was no longer conscious of the aromatic properties of son-of-a-gun stew. His lean face sober, he said, "You sure about this, Reb? I mean, you're not just feeling sympathetic towards the miners, are you? You have a tendency to side with the have-nots against the haves, you know, and it's quite obvious that you don't care for Kingston."

"Mebbe Kingston ain't my speed, but that don't have nothin' to do with this." Brazos leaned on the table, big slabs of muscle rolling under his shirt. "Yank, do you know there was five accidents in the Motherlode in two months afore the miners quit? And that eleven men were killed and another half dozen crippled?"

"No, I didn't …" Benedict's fingers tapped on the oilcloth. After a thoughtful minute he said, "This is sobering. Reb, quite sobering."

"Sure it is. Look, Yank, I understand as how you feel you gotta help Kingston on account of the past, and damn it all, I been ready to stand at your shoulder like I done yesterday. Kingston was your friend and needed your help, fair enough. But I dunno about you now. For my part I don't have much stomach for ridin' gun for Kingston—not since I know what's been goin' on down that mine, damned if I do."

Benedict was silent as he watched a freighter swing wide into Johnny Street. The mule team plodded past, almost invisible in the dust they kicked up, with a red-faced man in a cabbage tree hat trotting alongside the lead team and the driver standing and cracking his long whip from the wagon.

Benedict's manner was more decisive when he turned back to Brazos. "You're not suggesting we switch horses, are you?"

"Hell, no. I mean, you're in Kingston's debt … it wouldn't be fittin' to turn against him." Brazos fiddled with his coffee spoon. "I'm wonderin' if mebbe we oughtn't just up stakes."

"Quit?"

"Yeah."

"No. No … I came here to square an account and I'm staying until I do."

"But what about the mine and them fellers?"

"Reb, perhaps Kingston isn't lily-white, but neither are the miners. You can't tell me that big Clancy isn't bad news—and don't tell me it wasn't the miners behind the bullet that killed Bowers."

Brazos nodded. "You got a point there. But Clancy ain't really the miners' leader, you know."

"He seems to think he is."

"He walks plenty tall, sure. But I found out from Delaney that most of the workers only go along with Clancy on account they're too scared not to. Delaney hates his guts, and so do a power of others, he says. He reckons Clancy's got only about thirty hot-head supporters out of over a hundred miners. Delaney says he might have come to terms with Kingston before this, only Clancy don't seem to want to, no matter what."

Benedict frowned in thought. "That doesn't seem to make sense. What could Clancy gain by trying to keep them out of work indefinitely?"

The tortured corrugations that came to Brazos' forehead advertised that he found heavy thinking was required here. "Not even Delaney seems to know the answer to that, Yank. And, listen—this is mighty queer, too. Delaney tells me they would have been starved into goin' back to work long afore this, only Clancy's been antein' up for their grocery bills at the store."

"Clancy? But where would that overgrown son get that sort of money from?"

"Delaney says he ain't sure, but he's got a hunch the dinero comes from that jasper that owns the Silver King Saloon."

"Ace Beauford?"

"That name mean somethin' to you, Yank?"

Taking out his cigar case, Benedict selected a Havana and said, "Kingston's wife is having an affair with Beauford."

The hand lifting Brazos' coffee cup stopped half-way. "She what?"

A match burst into flame and touched the cigar into life. "Late last night, Mrs. Kingston left the house alone. I was curious, so I followed her to the Silver King and there observed her, shall we say, in flagrante delicto."

"In what?"

"In bed with Ace Beauford."

"Well, I'll be a dirty name."

"Exactly."

Benedict drew deeply on his cigar, tilted his head back and blew a perfect smoke ring at the ceiling. "So now I discover that the industrious Mr. Beauford is not only cuckolding my erstwhile comrade-in-arms, Foley Kingston, but seems to be involved with Clancy and the strike that might end up ruining Kingston." He ashed the cigar carefully. "Curioser and curioser, one might say."

"I don't get it," Brazos said. "I don't get any of it."

"I'm not sure I do either." Benedict glanced at his watch and rose. "Right now, Foley is expecting me for lunch. Coming?"

Brazos shook his head. "Reckon I'll mosey along to the Silver King. Somehow, sudden like, I need a drink." He got to his feet as Benedict spun a coin onto the table. "You goin' to say anythin' to Kingston?"

"Not my place," Benedict replied, giving the plump little waitress a flashing smile as they left. "Foley's private problems aren't my concern, just his public ones."

Sunlight struck yellow fire from the cartridge casings in Brazos' shell-belt as they halted on the edge of the gallery.

"So we just keep on like before?"

"That's right. Kingston expects trouble when he brings the strike-breakers in and doubtless he'll get it. I intend to see him safely through that, by which time I will consider our account squared. Then we can move on."

Brazos made no reply. Benedict started to move off, then paused. "I can count on your continued support I take it?"

A gusty sigh came from Brazos' barrel chest. "Sure, why the hell not?"

"Good." Benedict nodded and went down the street, a tall, long-striding figure that drew scowls from the men and sighs from the women.

Another windy sigh, and Hank Brazos hitched at his shell-belt and stepped down from the porch to cross the street. As he did, someone called his name and he turned to see Tricia Delaney hurrying along the walk with a shopping basket and a midget brown bull.

Brazos' blond eyebrows went up as he realized it wasn't a midget brown bull trotting at the girl's skirts, but Bullpup. The dog looked as if he'd rolled in dust, sand, tumbleweed, horse droppings, sawdust and maybe a few gallons of wet fertilizer.

"*Really,* Hank," the girl said critically as he came back and passers-by drew up to stare curiously at the filthy hound. "I thought you were a man who cared about animals. How on earth could you let your dog get into this condition?"

"I ... well—"

"I found him wandering along Bonanza Street coming from the corrals, so I brought him along with me, hoping I might see you." Tricia bent and patted Bullpup's iron skull. "There, there, he's a naughty man for neglecting you, isn't he?"

Bullpup looked pitiful. Brazos looked stunned.

"But you don't understand, Tricia. I—"

"I'm afraid I don't have time to chat at the moment, Hank," she cut him off, "but you will at least clean the poor little thing, won't you?" She waved as she went off. "Sorry I must rush. 'Bye, Bullpup."

"Poor little thing," Brazos gritted, fixing the dog with a look of absolute malevolence. "Why you simperin', smirkin', four-flushin', rump-sprung, liver-speckled, yellow-eyed mongrel, a man oughta—"

He broke off because Bullpup was wagging his stub of a tail and his yellow eyes were twinkling. After a while Brazos' scowl got too hard to hold, finally melting altogether.

"All right, you old kitchen thief," he grinned. "Come on and I'll throw a bucket of water over you. Then I'll buy you a beer."

SEVEN

THE FIGHT

Tobacco smoke and gloom were thick in the air of Ace Beauford's private office behind the Silver King Saloon as Holly Doone opened the door to Paddy Clancy's knock.

"What's wrong?" Clancy demanded. "What'd you send for me for?"

"Good morning, Clancy," Beauford said, underlining the greeting.

The huge Irishman flushed. "Sorry," he muttered. "'Mornin', Ace. 'Mornin' to you, too, Holly."

"Howdy, Clancy boy," drawled Holly Doone, Ace Beauford's gunfighter-bodyguard. He was a hawk-faced young killer with a bright banner of yellow hair, a natural quick grace and the reputation of being the quickest hand with a six-gun in town. "Drink?"

"Give him one," Beauford instructed. "I think he might need it."

Clancy didn't like the sound of that. He accepted a large whisky from Doone, leaned his powerful back against the wall while the gunslinger refilled Beauford's glass, and waited.

Beauford wasn't a man to be hurried. Swirling the whisky in his glass, he took a sip, then spun his swivel chair to peer through the spy slot in the wall that commanded a full view of the bar-room. There were more customers than usual for this time of day due to the fact that Spargo had a lot to talk about today.

The chair creaked as he turned to Clancy. Beauford was something of a mystery man to most of Spargo, despite the fact that he'd been operating the town's biggest saloon for almost a year. A lot of rumors were spread about him, but nobody seemed quite sure if he were sinner or saint. About all they were unanimous about, was that he was well-heeled and not a man to cross.

"We're in trouble," Beauford said in a flat voice.

"What kind of trouble?"

"Strike-breaker trouble."

"Strike-breakers!" Clancy made it sound like a curse. It was a word that had been circulating in strike-torn Spargo so long that most believed it to be just a rumor put about by Kingston to frighten the men back to work. "You've heard somethin' definite?" Clancy asked.

"Yes. Kingston is going to bring cheap Mexican labor up from Granite." Beauford paused for emphasis. "Dollar-a-day labor."

"A dollar-a-day! I can't be for believin' it, Ace!"

"You can take it for fact."

"You mean you heard it from …?"

"Mrs. Kingston, yes."

"Why, the dirty, treacherous divil!" Mottled marks showed on Clancy's angry face. "He's had this in mind right along—that's why he wouldn't even talk about re-timberin' the Motherlode."

"I'd say that'd be exactly right."

"Well, I'll be bunched and banjaxed." Clancy took two strides across the room, two back, then halted before the desk. "What'll we be doin' now, Ace? We can't let 'im bring 'em in."

Every mining man in Spargo would have been surprised to hear Paddy Clancy deferring to Ace Beauford. Not two-fisted Clancy who sought or accepted guidance from no man. But then, nobody but the three men in the room and Rhea Kingston knew how it was with Paddy Clancy and Ace Beauford.

It had begun several months ago when Beauford, already involved with Foley Kingston's bored wife, had first recognized the possibilities of the worsening relationship between Kingston, with his profit-at-any-price policy, and the unhappy miners who were doing the hard work and the dying for him. Encouraged by

Rhea, whose boredom with her husband had become outright hatred, he had set out to acquire both Kingston's wife and wealth. The best way to achieve his twin goals would be to help fan the flames of dissent in Spargo and aim for Foley Kingston's financial ruin … and then, when the time was right, the death of Kingston.

That was where Clancy fitted in. Adverse to hard work and ambitious to control men and affairs, Clancy was the perfect tool to help Beauford gain his ends. Clancy was sometimes violent and unpredictable, but it was through him that Beauford had begun the strike, and it was through Clancy's standing among the miners that Beauford, with the help of his own money, had been able to keep it going.

Until a week back, Beauford had been content to sit back and wait. There was a good chance that Kingston would be killed in a clash with the miners. If not, then Beauford would arrange an assassination. He'd hoped for the former, for after Kingston's death he planned to marry Rhea and take over the Motherlode and he didn't want any taint of suspicion concerning Kingston's demise connected with him if it could be helped. Once he was at the helm, Clancy would get the men back to work as mines manager, and Beauford would grow rich.

That was how it had been unfolding. But the first cloud appeared with the report that Kingston was importing a fast gun. Young Tommy Murphy had pestered them to let him make a try for Benedict's scalp and Beauford and Clancy had finally agreed to an ambush. But it hadn't worked out that way and Brazos and Benedict loomed to create a large problem indeed—a problem compounded by Kingston's plan to bring in cheap labor.

But Ace Beauford wasn't about to fold. He was a good enough gambler to grow rich from the profession, and he had put too much in this pot to drop out of the game. He was ready, if needs be, to shoot for the limit, winner take all.

He said, "It's pretty simple to figure out how Kingston's mind has been working. He wanted to bring the strike-breakers in all along, but he didn't dare to because he knew the miners would go loco. So he brought Benedict and Brazos in and now he figures he can do what he likes. Not bad planning …"

"So we'll crown Kingston a genius," Clancy snorted, unable to hold back his sarcasm and mounting frustration. "Now what?"

Beauford was about to reply when one of his dealers hurriedly entered the office to tell him that Duke Benedict's partner, big Brazos, was outside in the bar.

Swiftly, Beauford and Clancy crowded to the spy hole, with Holly Doone trying to peer between their heads. It wasn't difficult to pick Brazos out—his size and his purple shirt and the big dog standing beside him at the bar made him the Silver King's most conspicuous customer by a street.

"Look at him, will ye?" Clancy said venomously, unconsciously rubbing his bruised jaw. "He thinks he owns the place ... sure, just look at the way he's standin' there with—"

"I don't see Benedict," Beauford interrupted, his gaze sweeping the bar-room.

"And ye likely won't, for I seen the fop makin' tracks for Kingston Hill when I was on me way here," Clancy said.

Beauford turned from the slot and Clancy and Doone saw that the hooded black eyes were suddenly bright with purpose.

"We mightn't ever see them separated again," the saloonkeeper said, "so we've got to make the most of this."

"You mean—?" Clancy began eagerly.

"I mean we get him out of the way," Beauford snapped. "Now." He shook his head as Doone eagerly fingered his gun. "No. If we shoot him down cold, Benedict might start cutting loose and we're not ready for him just yet."

"But, Judas, Ace," protested Doone who'd been straining at the leash to take a crack at Benedict and Brazos from the start, "I could take that big jackass left-handed. I could—"

"I said no." Beauford turned his black eyes to Clancy who was smacking his fist into his palm. The murderous eagerness in the giant's eyes was a little frightening to see. "I think there's a better way … a surer way …"

"Name your poison, mister."

"Rye whisky," Brazos said.

"One rye whisky comin' up."

"And a dish of beer."

Turning away to get the whisky, barmaid Rosie Clinton blinked and turned back to the big man in the faded purple shirt.

"A dish of beer you said, mister?"

Brazos grinned. "Not for me. For him."

Rosie, a sturdy, good-natured woman of forty, leant over the bar and then pulled back quickly when she saw Bullpup staring at her with thirsty yellow eyes.

"It's all right, ma'am," Brazos assured her. "He's harmless."

"I'll have to take your word for that," Rosie said and went off to fill the unusual order. Returning with the whisky and the dish of beer, she watched curiously as Brazos set the dish on the floor and Bullpup commenced to lap into the beer with a hearty smacking of the tongue.

"Say, he really goes for that stuff, doesn't he?"

"At drinkin' or eatin' he's a natcherl champeen," Brazos announced proudly.

"Does he get drunk?"

"Only on the fourth of July and his birthday."

Rosie didn't know whether he was pulling her leg or not. She studied Brazos for a moment as he stood leaning against the bar sipping his whisky, then said. "You're one of them fellers that Foley Kingston brought in, aren't you?"

"That's right, ma'am." Brazos tipped his hat. "Hank Brazos is the name."

Rosie Clinton nodded soberly and looked around her. Two minutes before Brazos came in, the barroom of the Silver King had been filled with talk and noise. Now it was quiet with just about every eye in the place fixed heavily on the big Texan.

She said quietly, "I suppose you know most of the miners from the Motherlode hang out here, big boy?"

"Guessed it, ma'am," admitted Brazos, who'd seen little but blue denim since entering the saloon. "Anythin' special about that?"

Rosie, who had a soft heart, nodded. "Reckon so, big boy. I guess it wouldn't come as any surprise that you aren't exactly the most popular fellow around town with the miners. Just between you and me I think I'd be doing my drinking somewhere else."

"Why, thank you kindly for your advice, ma'am, but I reckon I'm comfortable here."

Studying him, Rosie wondered for a moment if he understood her warning. Then she saw the twinkling confidence in the blue eyes and realized that he just wasn't the type to scare easily. Taking a good second look at his wide shoulders, she understood why.

A customer called the barmaid away and Brazos pulled out his Bull Durham and commenced to build a cigarette. Facing the batwings, he'd just set the cigarette alight and was picking up his glass when somebody bumped him from behind, spilling his whisky. Brazos straightened. Standing before him, massive and scowling, was Paddy Clancy.

"Faith now and it's a careless man you are with your elbows in a bar-room, Mr. Gunfighter," the Irishman said. "You're like to knock the wind out of a man throwin' your arms about that way."

Sensing the threat in the man's voice, Bullpup bared his teeth but Brazos ordered him to sit. Looking past Clancy's massive shoulders, Brazos saw Ace Beauford and his gunfighter, Holly Doone, leaning against the bar ten feet away. Brazos felt the hair on the back of his neck rise at the smell of trouble.

"I'm waitin', lad," Clancy told him.

"For what?"

"Why, for you to be sayin' as how you're sorry for bumpin' me in the stomach, o' course."

Hank Brazos had been in too many bar-room brawls not to realize that Paddy Clancy was bracing him. And the crowd knew it, too, for now the Silver King Saloon was almost totally silent and every eye was on the two big men at the bar.

Brazos smiled easily and said, "I don't reckon as how I'll be apologizin', seein' as it was you that bumped me, Clancy. But just to show you there's no hard feelings, why don't you let me buy you a drink?"

Paddy Clancy's eyes glittered as he mistook the other's attitude for lack of nerve.

"You'll have to be excusin' me, for it's never been me habit to share a glass with dirty butcherin' gunfighters." Clancy smiled mockingly. "You can understand how I feel, can't you, lad?"

Brazos could feel his patience wearing thin, but he managed to keep a rein on his rising annoyance. There were times when he would gladly walk five miles for the prospect of a good drag out brawl. But that wasn't the case here. There was more than enough trouble in Spargo without him tangling pointlessly with big Paddy Clancy. So he scratched his navel, glanced at the batwings, sighed, drained his glass and straightened.

"Let's go, Bullpup."

"What's this?" Clancy growled as Brazos turned to leave. "We haven't finished our little bit of business, gunfighter."

"No business to finish as far as I'm concerned."

"What's the matter, Brazos? No guts?"

Brazos froze. He turned slowly, blue eyes like chips of steel. "I reckon I'll be askin' you to take that back, Clancy."

Delighted with the response his insult had brought, Clancy stood with his feet wide apart, massive hands hooked in his three-inch-wide leather belt.

"Oh, I'm a frightened lad and no mistake." His face turned scornful. "Gunfighters! I never seen one yet that was a man. Back home in old Ireland, the only feller you'll ever see carryin' a gun is some underfed little imitation of a man that don't have the stomach to fight fair. I guess that's how it is with you, gunfighter, big as you are."

Brazos glanced at the batwings. He knew he could still walk out on this. But, looking back at Clancy and the silent, expectant crowd, he realized that if he backed down to Clancy now, there was no telling where it would end. So far he and Benedict had managed to keep on top of the game here in Spargo, but that could fall apart quickly if they were to lose their hard-won respect. Were he to back away, others might interpret it as a sign of weakness and it would only be a matter of time before somebody else tried to take him down another peg. With the odds so heavily stacked against them in Spargo, that wasn't something they could allow to happen.

Brazos came slowly back to Clancy, weighing him up with an expert eye. It wouldn't be easy, he calculated—then suddenly he wasn't thinking of anything as Clancy laughed and spat in his face.

Brazos' blurring right fist caught the giant square on the jaw and sent him staggering. For a moment astonishment showed on Clancy's rugged visage. He'd felt the enormous power behind that punch. Then with the excited shouting of the crowd in his ears, Clancy cocked his fists professionally, stepped in lightly with a left to Brazos' ribs, then caught him hard on the shoulder with a booming right that almost knocked him off his feet.

The Silver King was a silent arena as the combatants circled each other warily. Brazos' blue eyes were no longer lazy, and Clancy was grinning behind his fists.

Suddenly Brazos attacked. Moving swiftly he slid away from a left and went through Clancy's guard to connect with a whistling straight right to the nose that drew crimson. He followed with a booming left rip to the ribs that made a sound like an Apache war drum, then he ducked low as Clancy roared and swiped a wicked hook at his head.

The hook missed but a ripping uppercut that seemed to come from nowhere didn't. Brazos found himself staggering back, his vision clouded. Ducking instinctively, he felt another blow whistle past his ear. He shook his head desperately to clear it and then, as Clancy came in again, he grabbed the Irishman and clinched.

"Ah, beginnin' to feel the weight of Clancy's fists already are ye, gunfighter?" Clancy mocked.

With a burst of power, Brazos broke away, punched both fists hard to the face, then switched his attack to the mid-section and sledged in three quick rips.

"You can't be hurtin' me there," Clancy boasted, then sent Brazos back ten feet with a straight left that had the kick of a pile-driver.

Shaking his head, Brazos came back into it and for a brutal minute they stood toe-to-toe slugging it out with the excited roar of the spectators threatening to lift the Silver King's roof. Both men were bleeding as first one, then the other, seemed to get the upper hand. Brazos was incredibly strong, but it seemed to the experts in the crowd, including Beauford and Holly Doone, that Clancy was surely getting on top.

It was beginning to seem that way to Brazos, too. He'd never encountered a man of Clancy's strength. He seemed almost to enjoy the crash of knuckles against his big head and rock-like body, and his blows seemed to be picking up power as he went along.

"Ah, you poor fool, Brazos!" Clancy panted glee-fully as a sledging right to the mid-section had Brazos hanging on again. "You weren't for knowin' that I'm goin' to kill you, were you?"

The threat penetrated Brazos' numbed senses. Staring at Clancy from behind the protection of his fists as he backed away, he realized that the man meant what he said. This wasn't just a test of strength—Clancy was trying to kill him!

The awareness that he was fighting for his life and not just a victory sent a fierce flood of strength surging through Brazos' battered body. Feigning weakness, he half stumbled as the bullocking Clancy caught him with a glancing left. Clancy swallowed the bait and dropped his guard as he attempted to cripple Brazos with a kick. Brazos dodged the boot and came back in like an express train, butting to the jaw with his head, punching to the heart and kneeing to the groin all in one smashing assault.

Clancy looked hurt for the first time in the fight, pain and astonishment showing clearly in his face. Snarling, he threw himself at Brazos and wrapped a headlock around his neck, trying to reef him off his feet. When that failed he threw him on a table, smashing it to fragments. Snatching up a broken table leg, he swiped at Brazos' head as he bounced to his feet. Ducking, Brazos dived low, seized the giant's legs and heaved. The saloon shook to its foundations as Clancy crashed down. A lashing boot caught Brazos square in the guts as he made to leap on his downed opponent. He staggered back, tripping over the broken table. Clancy got half erect and dived at him, but Brazos swung up both feet to catch him in the belly. Clancy roared wildly as he flew through the window, hit the porch with a mighty crash and rolled into the street. Dazedly, he struggled to his feet as Brazos came lunging through the batwings with a mass of excited spectators behind him.

It wasn't over yet.

EIGHT

BENEDICT'S GUN

The exploding window and the roar of the crowd drifting up from the town below gave Benedict his first intimation of what was going on in Johnny Street as he came down the hill from the Kingston mansion. Upon reaching the house, he had been told by Rhea that her husband had gone to the mine and had left a message for Benedict to wait for his return.

Rhea had seemed quite happy to sit and talk with him while he waited. But after what he'd seen last night, he didn't feel comfortable in the woman's presence and so had elected to head back to town with the intention of returning to the house later.

Now, halfway down the hill, Benedict halted. Squinting his eyes against the sun's glare, he saw the turmoil of activity in front of the Silver King Saloon. With the dust it wasn't possible to see exactly what was going on, but a lot of people were milling about down there and more were running to swell the crowd.

Curious, Benedict strode quickly down the trail. As he reached Johnny Street, he heard somebody running towards the Silver King shouting, "Fight!"

But it wasn't until Benedict reached the perimeter of the crowd and caught a glimpse of Paddy Clancy and then a faded purple shirt that he realized who was putting on the show.

His first reaction was one of disgust. Surely to hell Brazos had enough sense to realize that this wasn't the time and place for stupid brawls.

But, as Benedict climbed onto a parked buckboard to get a better view, he saw the combatants and knew this was no ordinary brawl. There was a murderous ferocity to the blows these men were slamming into each other as they stood toe-to-toe in the dusty center of the excited crowd in the street before the saloon.

Brazos was bleeding copiously and Clancy looked even worse. One of his eyes was shut tight, there was a gap in the front of his mouth where teeth had been, and Benedict could hear the tearing rasp of his breath from fifty feet away.

It looked to Benedict as if Brazos was getting on top.

It seemed that way to Paddy Clancy, too, as still another straight left made contact with his battered face and knocked him back against the rear wheel of a freighter wagon. Clancy couldn't believe it. Even after he'd taken the header through the window, he'd still felt he had Brazos' measure. But in the wild minutes since, Brazos had pounded him mercilessly and was still quick enough to dodge two out of every three punches Clancy threw.

Never before had Clancy faced the prospect of defeat. Victor of a hundred brutal brawls, he was yet to know the ashy taste of running second. He couldn't let himself lose, not here in front of the whole town— and not to Hank Brazos. Everything he'd built in Spargo was based on the power behind his two fists. It was an authority he had to maintain or sink back into the ranks of mediocrity.

Desperation made him crafty. He'd learned a thing or two from Brazos about feigning weakness. Pushing himself off the freighter wheel, he took a tremendous roundhouse swing, missed and fell to his hands and knees.

A great gasp went up from the crowd. Everybody thought he was finished.

"Damn it, Brazos got the better of him," Beauford hissed, but when he turned to see why Holly Doone didn't answer, he saw that Doone was no longer standing at his shoulder.

Doone was in the crowd peering between the shoulders of two miners at the fallen Paddy Clancy. There was a lethal light in his eyes and he was fingering the butt of his .45.

Brazos waited for ten seconds for Clancy to get up, then he panted, "Had enough, tough mouth?"

Clancy's bowed head nodded. His chest heaving, Brazos turned slowly away. Just as he did, Clancy's great hands lashed out, wrapped around his ankles and jerked him off his feet. Clancy then clapped a stranglehold around Brazos' neck.

"Thought you had me, didn't you?" he cried triumphantly. "You poor fool. No man beats Clancy."

For a bad moment the street swam in Brazos' vision as Clancy's forearm mangled his windpipe. But then, with a desperate effort he twisted and locked his hands around Clancy's waist. The stranglehold was still in place, still so fierce that Brazos couldn't see, but now he was applying force, bending Clancy's great torso back.

The crowd fell silent as the terrible test of strength moved towards a climax. Both men were kneeling, Clancy with his massive arms squashing Brazos' throat, and Brazos arching Clancy's body back inch by agonized inch from the waist. Locked that way, they formed an awesome tableau for a full minute and then somebody whispered:

"Clancy's goin'!"

But Clancy was already gone. The arms around Brazos' neck didn't have the strength to crush an egg. For just a moment, as he felt the giant's bones turn to water in his hands, Brazos was tempted to push back that extra inch which would have snapped Clancy's

112

spine. It was surely what Clancy would have done had their positions been reversed, but, reminding himself that he wasn't Clancy, Brazos unlocked his grip and let his adversary fall to the street.

It was then that Holly Doone made his play. Inflamed by the blood and violence and angered by Beauford's refusal to let him take care of Brazos in the first place, the young killer slid his six-gun from leather.

The slight dip of Holly Doone's right shoulder might have seemed insignificant to most people, but not to Duke Benedict. During the time he'd been watching the ruckus from the buckboard, Benedict had been keeping a sharp eye on Beauford and Holly Doone. What he'd seen at the Silver King last night, backed up by his discussion with Brazos earlier, made Ace Beauford highly suspect, and Beauford's expression as he watched Clancy losing ground had been deadly ... but now it was Doone who was making a play.

Benedict's reaction was the instinctive, lightning move of a man who knew the life-or-death value of a split second. He drew and fired in one fluid motion. His bullet found its target an instant before Doone could squeeze the trigger.

A roar of panic went up from the crowd as the shot rocked the street. The bloody combatants were forgotten as people knocked each other down in a scrambling effort to get out of the line of fire.

As the crowd parted, Benedict was revealed in clear sight on the buckboard, a smoking Colt .45 in his fist. Face-down in the dust where he'd rolled off the side-walk, was Holly Doone.

His chest still heaving, Brazos turned slowly away from Clancy, his eyes narrowing with comprehension as he, like all the staring onlookers, saw the naked Colt in Holly Doone's fist.

"He intended to do what Clancy was unable to, Reb," Benedict said grimly. Then he jumped to the ground and approached the gallery where Ace Beauford stood looking stunned. "This your idea, Beauford?"

Beauford shook his head. "No …" He stared down at the dead man. "Damned fool …"

"Dead fool," Benedict amended, housing his gun. He turned to Brazos. "Come on, Reb. We'll—"

"Just a moment … we ain't for bein' finished with this yet."

They turned to see that Clancy had regained his feet. He looked as if he'd lost an argument with a buzz-saw, but to their astonishment, he was lifting his fists in a fighting stance.

"Ah, don't flog a dead horse, joker," Brazos said disgustedly. "Goddamn it all, a man's just been killed."

"We ain't finished yet," Clancy mouthed, shuffling around him. "Come on, damn you."

It was impressive but pathetic. Paddy Clancy, it was plain to all, couldn't have licked a stamp in his condition.

Then an imperious voice sounded from the crowd and a skinny little woman in a black dress and bonnet came through and walked fearlessly up to Clancy.

"Come on, there's been enough of this foolishness, son."

Clancy dropped his fists. "But, Mother, you can't be for stoppin' me before I've—"

"I said there's been enough of this foolishness," Mother Clancy repeated. "Just look at ye, all covered with blood and dirt ... and not a lick of respect in ye for a man that's dead!"

"But, Mother—"

"Enough," tough little Mother Clancy snapped, and reaching up, seized her giant son by the ear. "If ye got no more sense than a child, then I'll be treatin' ye like a child. Come on, we're goin' home."

Perhaps it was a funny sight, a gray-headed little woman leading a bone-crushing giant like Clancy away by the ear. But nobody laughed. Spargo seemed to have had its fill of fun for one day.

"Will you please sit still for a minute, Hank Brazos?"

"Look, I feel fine now, Tricia. Honest."

"Men!" the girl said in mock disgust, dipping the cloth in the bowl of water and laudanum on the kitchen table, then reapplying it to his face. "I'm sure I don't know what you'd do with yourselves if it wasn't for us women. You don't know the first thing about looking after yourselves, and that's for sure. I suppose you'd still be standing up there at the bar of the Lucky Cuss drinking beer if Dad hadn't met you and had sense enough to bring you home to get patched up."

Shamus Delaney chuckled from his place by the window as Brazos sighed in resignation. "They always know best, son," the Irishman assured him. "At least to hear them tell it they do."

"All I'm wonderin'," Brazos grumbled, wincing as the cloth touched a tender spot, "is if young Cole Kingston knows what a bossy woman he's gettin' himself mixed up with."

"Be still," Tricia said firmly, but she smiled despite herself.

Finally she was through. As she put the things away, Brazos got up and studied himself in the little square of mirror hanging by the kitchen cabinet. He was agreeably surprised. In the bar mirror at the Lucky Cuss, where he and Benedict had repaired for a few badly-needed whiskies after the showdown at the Silver King, he'd looked like twenty miles of bad road. Thanks to Tricia Delaney's skill, he now looked no closer than ten.

"You'll be stayin' for supper of course, Hank?" the girl said. "Steak and potatoes tonight."

"She makes the best creamed potatoes in Spargo, son," said Delaney, "and there's nobody fussier about potatoes than an Irishman, I can tell you."

"Well, I dunno if—"

"Of course you will," the girl decided for him. "Now you two go sit on the front verandah in the cool while I get supper ready."

"Real bossy," Brazos grumbled, but when he was out on the verandah with Delaney, he added, "A nice kind of bossy."

"She's a good girl and I'm proud of her, son," Delaney said as they sat down. "I only hope … well, I only hope nothin' ever makes her too unhappy."

"You mean the set-up with her and Cole?" Brazos asked as he pulled out the makings.

Delaney nodded, then watched the sky, crimson and gold above the setting sun. "He's a fine lad, Cole. Ten times the man his father is. He and my Tricia are just made for each other … still, I'm doubtin' if anything'll ever come of it the way things are in Spargo …" His voice trailed off, then he grinned. "But that's no problem of yours, son. Tell me, are you feelin' all right now?"

"Just fine," Brazos replied.

It was almost the truth. He couldn't recall ever having fought a harder man than big Clancy, but apart from aching ribs, a few tender spots on his face and eight well skinned knuckles, he was feeling almost chipper.

117

As they sat yarning and smoking the day gave way to night, then Benedict and Cole Kingston arrived. The two had met up the street, and when Cole told Benedict that he intended calling in briefly to see Tricia before going home, Benedict decided to come around and see how Brazos was recovering. Benedict spent ten minutes or so with Delaney and Brazos and was ready to leave when Cole did, but Tricia insisted that he too stay for supper.

"Well, that's very gracious of you, Miss Delaney," Benedict said, "but I think Mr. Kingston expects to see me tonight."

"He'll make out without you, I reckon, Yank," Brazos said, and he was glad when Benedict agreed to stay on. Benedict had had to kill a man today and only Brazos understood how that weighed down on him. Tonight, Benedict would be best off amongst friends.

When darkness came and Benedict hadn't arrived, Foley Kingston began to worry.

"Perhaps he was injured in that business at the Silver King," he said to Rhea as he paced restlessly up and down before her chair on the long white gallery.

"He wasn't hurt," Rhea said impatiently. "Jib Hilder was standing beside him. He said Duke shot Holly Doone down and that was all there was to it."

"Then why hasn't he shown up all day?"

"Perhaps he's down Coyote Street flirting with the girls. How would I know?"

A retort came to Kingston's lips but he bit it off. Not even Rhea's tongue was going to spoil today for him. Today had seen the vanquishing of Clancy and the elimination of the gunfighter, Holly Doone. He'd decided that Doone had joined forces with the miners. Yes, it had been a big day, even if he couldn't understand why neither Benedict nor Brazos had been to see him since the blow-up at the saloon.

When the night wind began to blow, Rhea went inside but Kingston remained alone on the gallery. Finally, Cole came riding through the gates.

"'Night, Dad," the boy said. He left his horse with Regulator Chick Hasty and climbed the broad marble steps. "Sorry I'm a little late. I, er, was held up."

"Never mind about that. Tell me, did you see any sign of Duke while you were downtown?"

"Matter of fact I just left him, Dad. Why?"

"Is he all right? I haven't seen him all afternoon."

"Sure, he's fine. Maybe a little shaken up after the sh—"

"Where is he?"

Cole Kingston sighed. He wished he could lie to his father, but he'd never learned the knack.

"He's at the Delaneys with Brazos."

"Delaney's? What in heaven's name is he doing there?" Cole shrugged. "Having supper."

Cole waited for awkward questions but they didn't come. At that moment, Foley's mind was occupied only with the fact that Benedict was breaking bread with the enemy. He didn't like that one little bit.

Leaving Cole looking wonderingly after him, Foley strode towards the stables shouting for Hasty not to unsaddle Cole's horse.

"You goin' ridin', boss?" the Regulator asked as he brought the horse back out.

"Of course I'm going riding," he snapped, taking the lines and swinging up.

"Well, just half a minute and I'll be with you, Mr. Kingston."

Riding with a bodyguard had become so customary with Kingston that he found himself sitting his saddle waiting patiently for Hasty. But then he realized that riding with a Regulator would amount to a show of fear. When he rode through town earlier he'd seen the miners, stunned and cowed, beaten in the wake of Clancy's mighty fall at Brazos' hands. Yes, today he'd tasted a heady victory and he meant to enjoy it to the full.

He would ride alone down to Bonanza Street. That would show them all that Foley Kingston knew he was firmly back on top.

NINE

CANCELLED DEBT

Egstrom was alone at the funeral parlor knocking up a coffin for Holly Doone. About seven o'clock, old Billy Murphy appeared in the doorway. The rusty old gun was stuck in his belt and a rye bottle poked from a coat pocket. His crutch was under his arm and his empty trouser leg was sewed like a sack across the bottom.

Something about the old man disturbed the undertaker. Perhaps it was the gun, or maybe it was because old Billy looked *really* crazy tonight.

"Something you want, Billy?" Egstrom asked.

Murphy crutched himself drunkenly across the room and stood staring down at Doone's body. "Me boy. They done me boy in …"

Egstrom gaped. "Your boy, Billy? But that's not Tommy. That's Holly Doone."

"Murdered me only son in cold blood they did," the old man mumbled. "They'll have to pay," he added, shaking his head and making for the door. "They'll all have to pay ..."

The undertaker went to the door and stared after Billy. "Crazy," he said. "Really crazy now ..."

Egstrom was right about that, but he didn't know the extent of Billy's madness—nor did anyone else. Nobody liked Old Billy enough to have noticed the rapid deterioration in his mental state over the past few days. Spargo had grown accustomed to his ranting and snorting and spouting out his hatred for Foley Kingston, and if he'd been talking a little wilder and drinking more than usual the last day or so, then they supposed he had a right, what with his son being killed. But after his son's death had come two days of savage drinking. This, plus the violent incidents at the Silver King that day, had finally snapped a brain long weakened by alcohol, pain and hatred.

Mainly it had been the defeat of Clancy that had done it. Of all the miners in Spargo, Clancy alone had the fury and the power that Murphy could look up to. In Murphy's half world of near insanity, Clancy had always been his hope, the one man who might bring down Foley Kingston's citadel. Clancy had been his rock, then Brazos had smashed the rock and something had gone in the old man's head. He'd seen Benedict shoot Holly Doone, but the recollection had become clouded through a day of drinking and brooding in his old frame house out by the cemetery. At times he saw Benedict shooting Doone, then it was Benedict shooting his son. Later he thought it had been Foley Kingston with the blazing gun and in the end Kingston and Benedict were inextricably confused. But the identity of the victim became constant. Every time he saw it again in his mind, it was his son going down in front of the saloon.

He turned into Chisum Street and made his way to a favorite spot, the gloomy porch of the old derelict hotel five doors down from Johnny Street. Lowering himself to the porch edge, he leaned his crutch against the wall and took out his bottle. The butt of the old gun stuck into his ribs and he straightened, then drank deep.

"Not a man amongst 'em!" he muttered fiercely, and belched.

People passed by but paid him no more attention than he did to them. And then, suddenly, a voice penetrated the fog around him:

"Howdy, Mr. Kingston."

Kingston?

Old Billy looked up sharply. A passer-by had halted nearby to greet a passing rider. The horseman passed a street light and he saw the arrogant, hated face of Foley Kingston.

The bottle dropped unheeded from Murphy's fist. He seized his crutch and came upright as Kingston rode slowly down Chisum towards Bonanza Street.

Murphy knew that only fate could have brought Foley Kingston to him, tonight of all nights. Benedict, he realized with a crystal-clear insight as he crutched swiftly after the unsuspecting rider, was only the tool of the devil. It was Kingston who'd crushed and burned all the poor lads in the mine. Kingston was responsible for poor Tommy's death. Poor Tommy … whose rusty old .45 felt like an extension of his own vengeful arm as he jerked the gun from his belt.

Brazos leaned back in his chair, patted his muscular midsection and smiled contentedly.

"Well, Yank, I reckon if my ole pappy was here tonight, he'd say to me, 'Son, if you're dumb enough to let yourself get into ruckuses with an Irishman the size of a grizzly bear, then the best thing you can do for yourself afterwards is to wrap yourself around steak and potatoes dished up by Miss Tricia Delaney.' You reckon he'd say that, Yank?"

"Your father would say anything." Benedict smiled as he turned to the girl. "But it really was a fine meal, Tricia."

"My pleasure, Duke. But you're not leaving so early, are you?"

Benedict had picked up his hat from the table. "I never like to overstay my welcome."

"Heck, there's hardly any chance of that," Shamus protested. "You've only been here an hour. Can't you be for stayin' and havin' a little game of cribbage with me and Hank? Hey, you're stayin' on, ain't you, Hank?"

"Well, I dunno, Shamus, I—"

"'Course you are," Delaney decided for him. "You're better off here playin' cards with me than trailin' your coat around town tonight. You're not goin' to get the rest and attention you can be gettin' here."

"Well, if you put it that way, I guess I'll stay on a little then," Brazos said. "How about it, Yank?"

"Thanks all the same, but I guess I'd better go see Foley now." Benedict shook hands with Shamus and turned to Tricia. "Thanks again for the fine meal. See you later at the hotel most likely, Reb."

"Take it easy, Yank."

Leaving the house, Benedict paused at the gate to light a cigar, then strolled slowly towards Chisum Street. Bonanza Street was quiet except for a couple of urchins playing near the old bakery, a domestic argument going on across the street, and a horseman just turning into Bonanza around the Chisum Street corner.

Benedict watched the rider absently, sensing that he'd seen the horse before. He felt relaxed as he puffed on his smoke, but he narrowed his eyes curiously as somebody came hobbling fast around the corner from Chisum Street. Suddenly everything jolted into sharp focus. The hobbling figure had a gun in his hand and was aiming it at the unsuspecting rider.

And the rider was Foley Kingston!

"Foley, look out!" Benedict shouted as he raked for a Colt.

His gun was still snaking out of the holster when Murphy's Colt exploded. From the corner of his eye he saw the horse going down and then he had the gunman in his sights. Recollection of Holly Doone going down under his gun earlier pulled his barrel a fraction off dead center as he squeezed the trigger. The gunman went down screaming, a bullet in the shoulder.

Cursing under his breath, Benedict sprinted down the walk to snatch up the dropped gun of Billy Murphy who writhed on the ground. Then he spun on his heel and ran to Foley Kingston, slowing with a sigh of relief when he saw Kingston getting to his feet. The horse was dead, but Kingston was unharmed except for a shaking.

"Duke," Kingston panted as Benedict reached him. "What the hell happened? Who is that?"

"Old Billy Murphy," Benedict supplied as people came rushing from their homes to see what was happening. "You all right, Foley?"

"Damned, murderous old goat," Kingston said. "Yes, I'm all right, Duke. Is he done for?"

"Wounded."

"Pity you didn't kill him. I'll have him shipped down to Granite to stand trial for this as soon as he's fit to travel. You know I had no idea he was coming up behind me. Only for you, Duke … by God, only for you I'd be a dead man right now."

That didn't really register with Benedict just then. He'd only done what he would have done for anybody. And there was no time to think about it for Brazos and Delaney arrived at that moment and it was necessary to explain to everybody what had happened.

It wasn't until an hour later, over a large whisky at the Lucky Cuss Saloon with Brazos, that the significance of what Foley had said and what had happened hit Benedict.

He'd saved Kingston's life.

For the first time since coming to Spargo, Duke Benedict felt he was breathing free air. Not from the start had he been happy riding with Foley, but he owed him.

Now the debt was cancelled.

Morning …

"But, Duke, surely you can't be serious?"

"I've never been more serious in my life, Foley. I'm leaving."

Foley Kingston shook his head in disbelief. Benedict had just told him of the decision he'd made last night in the bar-room of the Lucky Cuss Saloon.

"But … but I don't understand, Duke. You've done so much for me. Why leave just when we're getting on top?"

"I've never liked this deal, Foley, any part of it," Benedict said. "And after yesterday …"

"You mean the business with Holly Doone?"

"Yes."

"But surely you can't hold me responsible for that? I had nothing to do with it. What happened there was just an offshoot of the fight between Brazos and Clancy."

"Damn it, Foley, can't you see? If it hadn't been for you and Clancy fighting your stupid war, yesterday wouldn't have happened. There would have been no fight, in fact Brazos and I wouldn't have been here."

"Well, I'm sorry you feel this way," Kingston said stiffly. "I thought you sympathized with my problems here."

"Not for a minute. Not with yours and not with the miners'. This affair could have been settled over a table between reasonable men. In my opinion, you're as bad as Clancy."

Foley Kingston was white with anger now. "I never expected to hear this from a former comrade-in-arms."

"Foley, we fought to keep a country at peace. Men died fighting what you and Clancy have allowed to happen here in Spargo."

Kingston stiffened. His eyes went cold. "I think you'd better go. Go, damn you! I don't need you any-more! Foley Kingston doesn't need anyone!"

"Foley, I really don't think you've *got* anyone," Benedict murmured, then he left.

In his upstairs room at the Silver King Saloon, Ace Beauford poured a finger of bourbon from the decanter on the bureau, and downed it. His head ached and his hands were not quite steady as he pulled on a clean linen shirt and looked for a tie. He seldom drank much, but he'd tied one on yesterday after the brawl downstairs. The heat of noon didn't help his hangover any.

Tapping heels sounded on the verandah and one of his percentage girls appeared in the doorway, decked out in her Sunday best.

"Aren't you comin' to the buryin', Ace?"

"No, I'm not. Beat it."

The girl disappeared. He poured another jolt of whisky and looked into the mirror. Black eyes stared back at him, reflecting his contempt. Why should he attend Holly Doone's funeral? All Doone had done was make things awkward for him by getting himself killed.

He finished dressing and went downstairs to the barroom. The shutters were closed against the glare. To his left, the bar was lined with men's backs. They were miners and they were drinking in silence. Yesterday had been a bad day for them, too.

He nodded to the barkeep and the dealers, made his way to his usual table to the right of the batwings and signaled to the bar for two fingers of whisky. Then he dealt himself a hand of solitaire. When the bar-man came over with his drink he didn't look up. He frowned at the cards without thinking about them.

Benedict and Brazos.

Just the thought of them dried his mouth. He picked up his glass and sipped. Two jokers in the deck and it was the biggest game he'd ever played in his life. Could he have foreseen what effect their pres-ence would have on his big plans? He didn't see how. He'd thought himself cunning and ruthless enough to get rid of both, in time. If only Clancy had broken big Brazos' goddamn back—that would have left only Benedict to concentrate on.

If. He took another little drink, then lowered his glass as the doorway was filled by a bellowing Paddy Clancy.

"Hey, you boozin' bastards, anybody seen Beauford today?"

"Here," Beauford called, then looked puzzled as the giant swung his battered face towards him and approached with a jaunty step. Knowing Clancy's van-ity, he hadn't expected the Irishman to show his face around town after his beating by Hank Brazos, yet here he was looking downright jaunty. It didn't add up.

"Ace," Clancy said excitedly, "have you heard?"

"Heard what?" Beauford asked sourly.

"They're leavin'."

"Who?"

"Brazos and Benedict."

"What?"

"It's the sweet truth, St. Patrick strike me dead if it ain't, Ace, me bucko," the giant exulted, leaning across the table and squeezing his shoulder. "They've just been down Bonanza Street, sayin' goodbye to Delaney, and I seen 'em ridin' for the south trail meself with their bedrolls and all on their horses."

Beauford was incredulous. "But why? How come?"

"Listen and I'll tell ye, lad. I got it from Delaney himself. It seems that Benedict was only stayin' on with Kingston because he owed him a big favor from the war. Accordin' to Delaney, neither of 'em had much stomach for workin' for Kingston all along, and last night, when Old Billy Murphy tried to murder Kingston and Benedict stopped him, Benedict decided he'd squared accounts with Kingston and told him he was leavin'."

"I can't believe it." Beauford's voice trembled with suppressed excitement. "Just when things looked worst, just when Doone got shot and—"

"I know, I know," Clancy said. Then, leaning close: "You know what it is, o' course, Ace—it's destiny, that's what. We've had a reprieve and we daren't tempt fate again by shilly-shallyin' another day."

"What do you mean?"

Clancy's eyes glittered. "I mean we strike, Beauford, today." He lifted his huge hands before him and made fists of them. "I mean Kingston, man. We can't be takin' another chance now that good fortune has smiled on us. We've got to do what I've wanted to do all along—squash him. You see that, don't you?"

Beauford smiled. Clancy was right. They couldn't afford to give Foley Kingston breathing space. With Benedict and Brazos pulling out, they had an unexpected opportunity that they dare not pass up.

Clancy jerked his head towards the miners at the bar. "We got an army ready for us, Ace. Them. A bellyful of your whisky on the house, a dose of Paddy Clancy's silver tongue—and I'll be a surprised lad if we don't have a full-scale riot on our hands. It wouldn't even surprise me if the lads got so worked up by tonight that they marched on Kingston Hill."

Staring into the giant's eyes, Beauford thought of Rhea Kingston with a sudden hot desire, and then he knew that his decision had been inevitable from the moment he'd set eyes on her.

"Jake!" he called across to his head barkeep. "You can close the till. No miner's dollar is any good here today." He grinned broadly as the drinkers gaped at him in astonishment. "You heard right, boys. Line up and name your poison!"

TEN

THE GATHERING STORM

Ten miles south of Spargo, Cherry Creek cut in close to the hillside bank and ran a deep, clear green. On one side, the foothills curved up steeply towards the looming Bucksaws, but the trailside was lined with trees. Willows crowded a broad stretch of yellow sandy bank and sycamores with mottled white limbs arched out over a deep, quiet pool.

Only ten miles, but it seemed like fifty to Duke Benedict as he finished off saddling the horses and then watched Brazos mix up a batch of sourdough biscuits.

It had been Brazos' idea to stop off and make early camp when they came to the deep bend in the creek. Benedict had wanted to put more distance between them and the town with its dust and hate and smell

133

of death, but he knew it wasn't how far you went but where you went that mattered.

"Hungry?" Brazos grunted.

"Somewhat," Benedict said as he pulled out his cigar case.

Brazos mixed flour, baking powder, salt and sour-dough starter and worked it into a firm dough. Then he pinched off balls the size of walnuts, put them in the skillet that was greased with lard and set them in the fire. He inhaled deeply as the good smell of cooking biscuits rose, then squinted at Benedict who was staring absently across the creek.

"Chewin' it over in your mind ain't goin' to do no good, Yank."

Benedict frowned at him. "What?"

Brazos stood up and dusted his hands on his chaps. "You're broodin' over whether you done the right thing by quittin' Kingston. Well, forget it. You done right all the way."

"Perhaps."

"No p'raps about it." Brazos hazed a grin. "Let's face it, Yank, we like clean-cut causes. We don't shine when we ain't dead sure who's wearin' the black hat."

Benedict sniffed. "I don't like the feeling of leaving something unfinished."

"Well, I got information for you … that feud back in Spargo ain't goin' to be finished until more blood's been spilled, not with pilgrims like Clancy and Kingston callin' the shots."

"How long will those biscuits take?" Benedict asked.

"Half an hour. The delicate aroma gettin' to you?"

Benedict grinned. "I think it might be."

"My pappy always used to say that if a man can't be tempted by sourdough biscuits, he's dead."

"Well, that would be right then—your pappy never being wrong about anything in his life."

"That's about how he was." Brazos grinned and went down to the creek for water. He felt it was encouraging that Benedict was slinging off at his old man. Soon he'd get around to insulting him and criticizing his cooking. That would be a sure sign he was putting Spargo out of his mind.

It was late afternoon in Spargo and Tricia Delaney was sitting in her kitchen talking with Cole Kingston when unsteady steps sounded in the hallway. With a startled glance at Kingston, the girl hurried out to see her father lurching towards her.

"Father!" she cried, shocked. "You're drunk!"

"Not just drunk, my baby … stinkin' drunk … that's what I am …"

Cole Kingston came hurrying out and helped Tricia put her father to bed. Most women along Bonanza Street were accustomed to having brothers, fathers and sons coming home drunk, but Tricia Delaney had never seen her father really under the influence before.

135

"Father," she chided as she pulled a blanket over him, "what on earth made you get yourself in such a state?"

"Free … all free," Delaney slurred, squinting his eyes. Then: "Cole? That you, Cole?"

"Yes, Shamus, it's me."

A stricken look crossed Delaney's whisky-reddened face. He shook his head from side to side on the pillow. "It's not right … what they're plannin' to do. I … I drank his free whisky so I'd forget it wasn't right … but I still know it's not …"

"What's not right, father?" Tricia demanded. "What are you talking about?"

Shamus Delaney closed his eyes. He seemed to be wrestling with a bad dream. Then his eyes opened and they saw horror in them as he clutched at Cole Kingston's sleeve.

"Go warn your father, Cole—hurry! Tell him to leave—they're goin' to—goin' to …"

"Going to what, father?" Tricia said, alarmed as his voice faded off.

Struggling with the effects of the whisky he'd drunk to deaden his sensibilities, Delaney slurred and muttered unintelligibly for a while before a brief period of lucidity returned.

"Goin' to march on the hill, Cole. Clancy's been workin' 'em up to it at the saloon. Tell your pa … tell him …"

Shamus Delaney's head rolled and he was asleep. Exchanging horrified looks, Cole and Tricia went out and closed the door behind them. The girl's dark eyes were enormous with worry.

"Oh, Cole, what father said—could it be true?"

"I'm sure it is," Cole said grimly. He turned to her as they reached the front door. "I'll have to go tell Dad, Tricia."

"Of course you must, Cole." She kissed him. "But please be careful, darling. If there is trouble afoot, you could be in danger, too."

"Heck, the miners have got nothing against me, honey," he assured her, then he hurried down the path.

He was right about that—but it didn't mean he was out of danger. Whenever he visited Tricia Delaney, Cole left his horse around the corner at Goodpasture's Livery so his father wouldn't find out where he was. Now, as he swung around the corner, he came face to face with the Kellys—Dad, Sam and Joe Kelly, rough, hard-faced men, close friends of Paddy Clancy's. They'd obviously been drinking.

Cole went to step around them, but young Joe Kelly barred his way. "Now where are you goin' to in such a hurry, Kingston?" he challenged, red-faced and truculent.

"Ah, let the lad be, Joe," counseled Dad Kelly. "He's not the Kingston we're after."

"So, it's all true!" Cole exclaimed. A mistake. He turned to run but Dad Kelly grabbed him by the coat and Joe Kelly punched him in the jaw. Cole fell to his knees and tried to get up. Joe Kelly punched him again and he slumped, unconscious, to the walk.

"No!" Dad Kelly barked as Joe lifted a brass-heeled boot above Cole's head. "Leave him be."

"He's a Kingston, ain't he?" Joe said, but he lowered his boot.

"He's harmless," the family leader declared. "Still, we don't want him runnin' loose this night." He jerked his thumb. "Tote him home and lock him in the cellar till it's over."

The Kellys lived four doors past the Delaney house. Two minutes later, a stunned Tricia Delaney heard a commotion and looked out to see Cole Kingston being carried past by the Kellys, followed by some noisy urchins who thought it was some kind of game.

Her face a mask of shock, the girl rushed into the street. "Mr. Kelly, what's going on? What happened to Cole? Where are you …?"

"Go back inside," Dad Kelly snapped at her. "This is no concern of yours."

She gasped when she saw blood trickling from Cole's mouth. She clawed at Joe Kelly's arm. "Put him down, Joe. Please!"

Cole Kingston's left foot hit the walk as Joe Kelly released his hold to backhand the girl across the mouth, knocking her down.

"I said it's none of your affair, girl," Dad Kelly growled, looming over her as she knelt there, stunned, her hand against her face. "Go back home and stay there. We won't be doin' any harm to your fancy gentleman, even if he be a dirty Kingston."

Tricia got slowly to her feet and watched them carry Cole into the house. Her face ached from Joe Kelly's blow, but that wasn't what stopped her. She'd seen their faces. They were strangers.

She looked around her and Bonanza Street seemed unfamiliar, alien. Something raw and ugly was rising from the boards of Spargo and she was afraid.

She fought against her fear as she paused at her gate. Instead of going into the house, she hurried down to Coyote Street. There she encountered the same stench of fear. The town was fixing to erupt and she felt helpless.

Then she came to a sudden stop before Kate Warren's sporting house as a desperate idea hit her. She turned and peered south over the rooftops. Benedict and Brazos had left several hours ago, but they hadn't seemed in a hurry

It was a desperate hope, she told herself as she stepped from the path of a drunk staggering towards Johnny Street with a gun in his belt. Even if she caught up with them, it was unlikely that she could talk them into coming back to save the town.

A shot rang out in Johnny Street. It was only a drunken miner shooting at the sky, but the ugly report told the girl that even a slender hope was worth grasping at. If anybody could stop what was building up in Spargo, it was *they*.

The liveryman let her have Cole's long-legged buckskin. Without getting into riding clothes, Tricia Delaney headed the buckskin out of town, then lashed the horse into a gallop along the trail that Benedict and Brazos had taken south.

The riders swung through the tall gates, clattered across the yard and reined in at the house. Wiping his nose on his coat, Art Shadie swung down in the deepening dusk and Foley Kingston came out rolling the chamber of a Colt .45 along his forearm.

"Got 'em all, boss," Shadie said.

"I can count," Kingston grunted. He'd sent Shadie down to fetch the Regulators from the Motherlode when it became apparent that big trouble was brewing. He noted that the men looked tense and pale.

"Take up positions inside with the rest of the boys," he ordered. "Pick up extra ammunition in my study."

Dismounting, the Regulators disappeared inside the house. Kingston waited until they were out of earshot before turning back to Shadie.

"You see anything of Cole?" When Shadie shook his head, Kingston frowned thoughtfully for a moment, then said, "How does it look with the strikers now?"

"Not good, boss. They're still boozin' at the Silver King. I reckon there's no tellin' what's goin' to happen when they stop drinkin'."

Kingston moved a distance along the gallery to stare through the trees at the town. "How many do you calculate we might have to handle if they come?"

"No tellin'. But it won't be less'n thirty or forty." Shadie paused a moment. "Heavy odds, boss. Mebbe we'd better kinda disappear until they sober up and then—"

"No!" Kingston snapped. "If I show fear before those scum, I might as well throw in my hand."

A sudden racket erupted inside.

Kingston scowled. Then, hearing his wife's voice raised in anger, he strode into the house with Shadie at his heels. They went through to the foyer that gave onto the servants' entrance, where they found a furious-faced Rhea Kingston attempting to pull Regulator Jib Hilder away from the closed door.

"All right, all right, goddamnit!" Kingston shouted above the clamor. "What's going on here?"

"This—this mendicant refused to let me out, Foley!" Rhea blazed. "He even dared lay hands on me."

"I'm sorry, boss," said red-faced Hilder. "But you said that—"

"That nobody was to come in or leave without my permission," Kingston finished for him. "That I did, and you did the right thing, Jib."

"Just a minute—" the woman began furiously, but her husband cut her off.

"Dressed to go out, I see, my dear. You wouldn't have been running out on me, would you, just because things look a little uncertain tonight?"

Anger made Rhea Kingston's face ugly. She was doubly angry because Kingston had guessed what she had in mind.

"Foley," she said threateningly, "I don't have to tell anybody where I'm going or when—and that includes you. Now tell this ape to get away from that door."

"Sorry."

"What?"

Foley Kingston smiled at his wife, but the smile was as cold as sleet. "You're staying, Rhea. I've put up with your headaches and your locked door and your sharp-tongued bitchiness and your wandering around as you please for too long—but tonight you're staying where you belong. With me!"

Rhea's fury had drained away, leaving her face a sour cream color. She felt herself go weak in the face of Kingston's new strength and fear bit into her stomach.

"Foley," she panted, "you don't understand. You don't understand what's going to happen. You—"

She broke off, but it was too late. Kingston loomed before her, a hard, dry shine in his eyes.

"What *are* they going to do, Rhea?"

She didn't want to blurt it out, but fear had loosened her tongue. "They're going to burn the house down, Foley. We'll all be killed if—"

"Who told you?" She hesitated and his hand cracked across her face. "Who told you?"

"Foley—"

"Who?"

"Ace, damn you!" she raged. "Ace Beauford. He and Clancy are coming to burn you out and I hope they kill you."

"So …" Kingston smiled coldly. "It was Beauford. I knew there was somebody. But a dude gambling man? That's a come-down for you, Rhea."

"At least he's a man," she blazed. "At least he's not obsessed with money and power and—"

"Shut up!" he cried. "I don't want to hear about your grubby little affair." His eyes glittered. "I'll take care of Beauford when this is over."

Scorn twisted at her mouth. "You'll take care of Ace? You fool, he's going to take care of *you!* They're going to kill you, don't you understand that? They're going to kill the great Foley Kingston and I'm glad!"

Kingston staggered as if he'd been struck. "You want to see me dead?"

"Yes, damn you, yes!"

His face hardened. "You dirty tramp, I'll see—"

He broke off as Rhea made to rush past him. He grabbed her by the arm. She whirled and raked the side of his face with red nails. He punched her on the point of the jaw and she crumpled to the floor.

"You stay," he gritted out. "If I go down tonight, goddamnit you'll go down with me!"

His eyes jolted back into focus as he looked at Shadie. "Lock her in her room," he ordered and strode off. "Tie her up if you have to—but she stays."

"Right, boss," Shadie replied. Looking down at the unconscious woman who'd never missed an opportunity to belittle him and drive him crazy with her unreachable sensuality, he grinned and added softly, "With pleasure."

"Tricia!" Benedict breathed in astonishment, lowering his gun and stepping out from behind the willow tree as the girl rode into the fire glow on a lathered horse. "What in the world are you doing out here?"

Brazos appeared from behind a boulder on the opposite side of the camp where he'd taken cover at the sounds of hoof beats coming from the trail. Tricia sighed with relief and smiled at the big Texan.

"Oh, thank heaven it's you. When I saw your fire I prayed that it would be."

"What's wrong, Tricia?" Brazos said, holding her horse's head as Benedict helped her down. "You look kinda peaky."

Moments later, seated on a log by the fire with Benedict grave-faced at her side while Brazos poured coffee, Tricia told them what was happening in town.

"I know that none of this is really any concern of yours now," she said, accepting a tin mug of steaming black coffee from Brazos, "but I couldn't think of anybody else who could possibly stop this … this …" Her voice broke off.

"You just drink your coffee, Tricia," Brazos said quietly, then his eyes asked a question of Benedict.

Benedict stood and stared down at Tricia's dark head. He was silent for a while as he thought it out. He'd seen drunken mobs before and they were one of the ugliest sights on earth. He'd never have a sound night's sleep again if he were to turn his back on a town threatened by a mob.

They would go back. They had no choice.

ELEVEN

THE FIRES OF HATE

Suddenly they were ready. They'd drunk enough and they'd listened to Clancy enough and now they poured out into Johnny Street from the Silver King Saloon, forty drunken, dangerous men milling in the street, shouting loudly to each other as they turned their faces to Kingston Hill.

"We'll hang Foley Kingston to a sour apple tree!" one began to sing, and a dozen voices joined in the Yankee Civil War marching song with Kingston's name substituting for that of Jefferson Davis.

"Damnit, not yet!" Ace Beauford urged Paddy Clancy as they stood just inside the doors, watching. "Bring them back in for another round, Clancy."

"Sorry, lad," Clancy replied, flushed with whisky and violent excitement. "Not even I could be stoppin' them now."

"But Rhea still hasn't shown up. We can't—"

"She was supposed to be here an hour past, Beauford. I can't be for helpin' it if your fine lady friend has gone and changed her mind about you, now can I?"

"But Judas Priest, Clancy, you can't—"

His words were drowned out by a new chant from outside.

"Clancy, Clancy, show us the way!"

No longer aware of Beauford, Clancy shouldered his double-barreled shotgun, straightened mighty shoulders and strode out. He stopped on the verandah and their acclamation enfolded him like a wave.

"Clancy! Clancy! Clancy!"

It was his hour. Everything he'd worked and plotted for had led to this. Tonight Clancy would leave the ranks of mediocrity forever; tomorrow this town would be his.

"Wait, Clancy," Beauford shouted. But Clancy didn't hear. Bounding down from the gallery, the big Irishman shouted: "He's killed us by the dozens in his murderin' mine, boys, now it's his turn." He gestured dramatically towards Kingston Hill with his shotgun. "With Clancy, me lads! He'll show ye the way!"

They surged after him, their faces gleaming in the glare of the brands they'd lit. To those who watched in fear and horror as they tramped along Johnny Street, they were no longer forty individuals but a single, terrifying creature. A mob. A monster with leering eyes and wet, loose lips—heavy-footed, ponderous, powerful.

Transfixed with indecision, Ace Beauford watched them reach the bottom of the hill and begin to climb. Where the devil was Rhea? Why hadn't she come? He'd warned her to quit the house before dark. What had happened? Surely she hadn't changed her mind this late in the day as Clancy had suggested? But what other reason could there be?

They were half-way up the hill now. Beauford cursed, then jumped down to the street and strode after them. He searched for a familiar face along the crowded walks, but Rhea was nowhere to be seen.

The bullet aimed at Art Shadie came through the balustrade of the upstairs balcony and hit him in the heart. Throwing up an exploding rifle, he bent across the balustrade, hung there for a moment, then plunged down to the gravel drive below, the crash of his body drowned out by the savage cheers of the mob.

A smoking six-gun in each hand and sweat stinging his eyes, Foley Kingston saw Shadie go over the railing from his position at the far end of the gallery. He cursed bitterly. Shadie made three. The battle wasn't even ten minutes old and he'd lost three of his men. Only seven left.

Cautiously lifting his head over the marble railing, Kingston could see them closing in. They'd taken cover behind trees, fences and outbuildings when their first drunken charge had been halted by withering fire from Kingston and his waiting men, but now they were creeping in. Directly beneath him where two dead miners and a dying one lay in a bloody heap near the ornamental fountain, a bull-necked miner with a gun in one hand and a blazing brand in the other was crouching on his haunches, waiting for a chance to rush the house. Kingston lifted his gun, aimed, then ducked as lead snarled past his cheek. Bobbing up again, he saw the miner charging for the house. He ripped off three shots. The miner fell down, rolled, lurched to his feet and staggered on, his gun gone but still clutching the brand. Regulator guns roared from below and the miner fell again, but as he did he hurled the brand with desperate strength, through one of the living room windows.

Reloading his guns from his ammunition belt, Kingston peered down, waiting for the brand to be flung back out. It didn't appear. Chick Hasty was posted in the living room. Surely they hadn't nailed him, too? Perhaps the brand had gone out? But moments later the miners began to cheer and he saw the reflection of dancing flames on the ground.

"You can be sayin' your prayers if you know any!" roared the great voice of Paddy Clancy. "You'll be burnin' in this world and in the next."

"Remember Number Six Shaft, Kingston?" another voice shouted from the stables. "Remember Number Six, you murderer!"

Kingston licked his lips. Eleven men had died in a fire in Number Six Shaft at the Motherlode last year. Scum! A pity they hadn't all burned. Drunken Irish pigs!

He turned his head as Sump Conroy's head and shoulders appeared at floor level, in a doorway ten feet to his left. "We're burnin'!" Conroy shouted. "We got to get out!"

"We're going nowhere," Kingston snarled back, unable to believe the possibility of defeat at the hands of these men he despised so deeply. "Get down there and put the fire out."

"But, boss, it's—"

"Do as you're told or I'll blow your stupid face in." Conroy's ugly face vanished. Kingston turned his back to the yard just in time to see one-time Motherlode pump man, Brian Hoolihan, come rushing from the trees at the north end of the house waving a brand and shouting like an Apache. Kingston's gun bucked against the heel of his hand and Hoolihan was obscured in gunsmoke. When it cleared, he saw that the miner had fallen across his brand. Hoolihan jumped up with a terrifying scream, his clothes flaming. A gun snarled from below and the man spun and fell and burned, still screaming.

Kingston laughed. Of course they couldn't beat him. He rose and made for the door. He'd better see how his men were doing with the fire. Once that was under control, he could lead a counter attack. He'd suffered casualties but the miners had sustained heavier losses. And why not? They had no discipline, no real reason for fighting. He *did!*

The next thing he knew, he was sprawled across the step with a searing pain in his left side and the dim sound of cheering ringing in his head.

He'd been hit!

Bullets spattered against the walls and doorway as they tried to finish him off. Desperation gave him strength and he hauled himself to safety into a bedroom and kicked the door closed behind him. The door shuddered under the thud of bullets as he lurched out of the bedroom and gained the main upstairs corridor.

He examined his wound. The bullet had caught him in the side and gone right through. He was bleeding freely, but though he knew no real damage was done, the sight of his own blood had a strange effect upon him; it was as if he were bleeding away his courage.

Pulling himself together, he staggered to the rear balcony to see how Mack Hogg and Ed Rife were making out. He found Hogg lying dead, with a bullet in the head. Rife was gone.

A spasm of pain seized him. He pressed his hand to his side and lurched back inside as somebody spotted him from below. Chest heaving, gun in hand, he crossed the corridor again and caught the first smell of fire.

Squinting through a shattered window at the scene below him, Kingston felt the full wrench of fear. The voices of the miners down there belonged to men he'd victimized and exploited, now drunk on whisky and hate and smelling victory. Five minutes back, surrender had been unthinkable, now he realized it was impossible. They'd shoot him down like a dog if he asked for mercy.

Panic twisted his vitals and the impressive facade that had been Foley Kingston began to crumble as guilt and fear did their destructive work. His house was burning, his men were dead, and he was encircled by hate-filled miners, with Clancy and Beauford urging them on

Beauford!

Suddenly the flood of panic ebbed and he began to think like the old Kingston. There would be no dealing with Paddy Clancy ... but, Beauford? Did he have a last desperate card to play?

The idea caught hold of him. Not even aware of the pain in his side now, he ran along the corridor to the room where Art Shadie had lashed Rhea to her bed.

Ace Beauford, crouched in the gloom of the stables with Clancy and the Kellys, shouted with the rest as Foley Kingston fell. Another cheer rose moments later when flames burst from the living room and spread with incredible speed. A Regulator came running out with his hands above his head. A dozen guns stormed together and lead punched him all the way back to the flames.

Beauford grinned as the men cheered again. It was intoxicating, the feel of bloodlust and the taste of triumph. Victory was as good as his and the cost was only the lives of a lot of dumb miners who'd died happy because they'd died drunk.

Then he realized that the men beside him were shouting and pointing upward. Beauford lifted his gaze to the flaming upper gallery and his heart stopped beating.

Rhea!

"Beauford!" Kingston's voice carried down clearly. "Beauford, I'm coming out. Call off your guns or I'll kill her."

Beauford's heart constricted when he saw the terror in Rhea's face. Desperately he turned to Clancy and said, "Tell them to hold their fire, Clancy. We'll have to let him go—"

"Oh sure, sure we will, lad." Clancy grinned, then his face turned savage. "The devil we will! Open fire, boys!"

"No!"

Beauford's horrified shout was lost in the blast of the Kellys' guns and he saw Rhea sag as the bullets crashed home. There was a fleeting glimpse of Kingston as he let the woman fall and dashed back for the doorway, and then he too went down. On his knees, he struggled to rise, then vanished as a blazing section of roof collapsed onto him with a roar.

Beauford's eyes bulged from their sockets. Then, an incredible fury seizing him, he swung towards Clancy and raised his six-gun.

"You stupid Irish bastard," he raged. "You've killed her. You—"

Clancy wasn't about to deny it. And he wasn't through yet. Too late, Beauford realized that the double-barreled shotgun angling across Clancy's great chest was trained squarely on him. It went off like a field piece, filling the stables with a hellish blue light. Beauford made a gurgling sound like a man screaming underwater.

"Don't be thinkin' hard o' me, Ace, lad," Clancy drawled, cocking the second hammer. "I know you thought highly of the lass, and all I'm doin' is helpin' you be together again …"

"No," Beauford moaned, and Clancy snarled:

"Don't think I wasn't for knowin' all along that you were only usin' Clancy to help you get your strumpet and the mine, and then you'd be seein' to get rid of me, too, Beauford. Well, the laugh's on you, me lad."

"No!" Beauford cried again, and he died in a thunderclap as Clancy jerked the trigger again.

Riding hands and heels, Benedict and Brazos stormed across the Cherry Creek bridge. Their racing horses had outstripped Tricia Delaney and Bullpup by a full mile since they'd first seen the flicker of flames on Kingston Hill. Hitting Johnny Street, they thundered down its dusty length, scattering white-faced towners left and right. Other towners were streaming up the steep slopes of Kingston Hill—men, women, children, fit and infirm, some drawn by the smell of death, others by fear, and all by the spectacle of Foley Kingston's great mansion burning end to end.

Men cursed at the sound of galloping horses behind them, but they jumped aside when they saw who it was.

"Benedict and Brazos!"

The names swept through the surging, gaping mass of humanity like a brush fire in summer grass. It sped ahead of them, rolling through the trees and then across the blood-soaked yard above the crackle of flames and the shouting.

But the miners couldn't believe it. Sure and it was only some trick of the night wind and the crackle of flames that made them think they heard people calling those names.

Then the two horsemen swept through the gateway looking ten feet tall in the light of the flames. Brazos a terrifying giant with a rifle, Benedict a sort of avenging demon with twin Peacemakers glittering in his hands.

One glance at the scene was all it took Benedict to guess that they'd got there too late to help Foley Kingston. Bitter fury shook him as he bore down on the startled miners, a fury directed not just at them but at Kingston and everybody else who'd helped, through greed or hate or whatever, to make this bloody hour inevitable.

The dramatic appearance of Brazos and Benedict threw the miners into confusion. Not even the appearance of a cavalry column from Fort Hood could have shaken them more than these two who had made such an impression on Spargo in just a few memorable days. One man turned and ran and another flung his gun away—but one faced them with a roar of defiance, the double-barreled shotgun in his massive hands swinging upwards.

"To me, lads! To Clancy!"

His tremendous shout was engulfed in the roar of Duke Benedict's Peacemakers. Clancy's face fell open as the slugs wrote a bloody pattern across his chest. He staggered forward and a convulsive jerk of his finger discharged the shotgun, sending a howling stream of blue whistlers between the two horsemen.

Their guns spat in return and the earth seemed to shake when Clancy fell.

Dad Kelly cut loose and a hot slug fanned Brazos' cheek. Benedict fired once and Kelly fell on his back, kicking at the air. Firing between his horse's ears, Brazos knocked Joe Kelly down before he could use his Colt, then swung for another target but there wasn't any. Guns were hitting the ground, hands were lifting, eyes were gaping at the great dead figure of Clancy. It was over.

The hungry crackle of the flames seemed to grow louder after the guns fell silent. As a hundred pairs of awe-big eyes watched them from the safe distance of the wrought-iron fence, Brazos and Benedict dismounted. The gambler looked at the flames, then turned to one of the miners.

"Where are Mr. and Mrs. Kingston?"

The miner gestured at the inferno. "In there." Duke Benedict slowly holstered his guns.

Nobody felt much like food the next day, except the coffin makers and gravediggers Egstrom kept working late into the night. The day after wasn't much different, but on the third day, with things slowly beginning to return to normal, Terry Mulligan decided something special was called for to help folks take their minds off what had happened, so a handwritten sign appeared in the window of his eatery:

TODAY'S SPECIAL
SPARE RIBS WITH LONE STAR SAUCE

Brazos, insisting that he patronized Mulligan's establishment out of loyalty to Texas, put away three full ribs and enough Lone Star sauce to stun a goat.

Benedict, settling for one rib and a mug of coffee that Mulligan had thoughtfully fortified with a jolt of whisky, sat smoking at the front window table, while Brazos made up his mind whether he could handle a slab of Jalapeno pepper cornbread with his coffee. Outside, Bullpup dozed in the shade of the porch. The trail partners' horses stood patiently at the hitch rack, saddled and ready for the trail. The two men were pulling out as soon as Brazos felt he'd fortified his constitution sufficiently for the journey.

There was a subtle difference in the atmosphere today, Benedict noted as he watched the street. Under the eternal dust haze there was a feeling of optimism. A black chapter had closed and there was a rebirth of confidence in the future. Benedict smiled. The ability of people to pick up the strains of day-to-day living after great suffering was something he'd witnessed in cities ravaged by the Civil War. Seeing it happen here in Spargo brought an Old Testament proverb to Benedict's mind:

"As the whirlwind passeth, so is the wicked no more: but the righteous is an everlasting foundation."

Well, a whirlwind had certainly passed through Spargo, but now the righteous would build something solid and good on the ashes of destruction.

Brazos was just polishing off a last hefty slab of pepper cornbread when Tricia Delaney and Cole Kingston appeared in the street outside. The girl saw Bullpup and stopped to pat him. Benedict and Brazos got their hats, paid the check and went out.

"So you two are leaving?" Cole said, indicating the horses with a nod of his head.

"That's right," Benedict said with a bow and a smile for Tricia. "There is a cold trail we have to try and pick up." He peered into Cole's face and saw that the young man's look of uncertainty was gone; there was resolution, sureness, in his eyes.

"I've hired men to start re-timbering the mine," Cole said. "And I've cancelled the deal with the strike-breakers. All the miners will be back to work in a few days."

"We heard about it," Benedict said. "We intended to look up both of you to say goodbye."

"Go on and tell him," Tricia said impatiently as she tugged at Cole's arm. "Or are you too shy?"

"Tell us what?" Brazos asked.

"Tricia and I are going to get married," Cole said with a blush. "Soon."

Now Benedict was certain that Spargo would be all right. To his way of thinking, there was magnificent symbolism in the marriage of Foley Kingston's gentle

159

son and Shamus Delaney's beautiful daughter: a uni-
fying of the very forces that had torn the town apart.

A few minutes later, after congratulatory hand-
shakes with Cole and some premature kisses from the
bride, Benedict and Brazos rode across Cherry Creek
Bridge. Their last glimpse of Spargo was of the black-
ened ruins of the mansion on Kingston Hill.

Then the trail ahead beckoned and they urged
their horses into a gallop.